MW01121197

LAST STOP THIS TOWN

LAST
STOP
THIS
TOWN

DAVID H. STEINBERG

Monkey Business Press

Published by Monkey Business Press
Santa Monica, California

LAST STOP THIS TOWN Copyright © 2012 by David H. Steinberg

"A Decomposition" Copyright © 2006 by Jenna Lê,
used with permission of the author.

Book & Cover Design by Keetgi Kogan

This is a work of fiction. Names, characters, places, and incidents are the product of the
author's imagination or are used fictitiously, and any resemblance to actual persons,
living or dead, business establishments, events, or locales is entirely coincidental.

Summary: The last weekend before high school graduation,
as they prepare to go their separate ways, four life-long friends
spend a wild and raucous night in New York City that forces
them to face their fear of growing up... and growing apart.

ISBN-10: 1-46-990266-4 — ISBN-13: 978-1-46-990266-1
LCCN: 2012903793 North Charleston, S.C.

This book was typeset in Le Monde 10 pt. and Dynamoe.
Yearbooks entries were set in Adam's Hand, Easy Hand, Tiza, and zombieCat.

First Monkey Business Press trade paperback edition, 2012

Printed in the United States of America

For Keetgi

CHAPTER ONE

"ONE MORE WEEK."

The guys had known this day was coming since kindergarten. Hell, they'd been dreaming about it for years. As the day approached, the constant barrage of lame video-yearbook retrospectives and school newspaper top-ten lists forced them to think of little else. But now that high school graduation was actually upon them, they weren't so sure *how* they felt anymore.

But the one thing the four of them *did* know was how many days they had left in their high school careers. They probably knew how many hours. So when Dylan Glasco said "one more week" from behind the wheel of his blocky metallic orange Scion xB (known unimaginatively around school as the "Cube"), he wasn't trying to deliver some big newsflash. He was just trying to break the mind-numbing boredom that came with growing up in the suburbs.

Dylan himself was the type of guy who could front an emo band, if

he could sing, which he couldn't. He had a vintage Zac Efron thing going on with his hair, which might have rankled the homophobically-
inclined if Dylan weren't constantly having sex with beautiful teenage
girls. Growing up tall and good-looking led to success with girls, and
years of positive reinforcement had given Dylan confidence. But Dylan
never used his power for evil (as least not usually). It's like Sarah always
said, Dylan knew he was good-looking but he wasn't an asshole about
it.

Riding shotgun was Noah Scott, Dylan's serially-monogamous
wingman and boyfriend to the aforementioned Sarah. It wasn't that
Noah didn't have the looks to be a player. He could have worked his
nice-guy routine and dimpled cheeks into some serious tail if he'd wanted to. He just preferred to actually get to know girls before he hooked
up with them. Then, for reasons Dylan never understood, Noah liked to
keep hooking up with that same girl, over and over. "It's called a relationship," Noah explained to Dylan.

The Cube was parked in the McDonald's parking lot, as usual. The
four seniors were eating the remnants of their after-school grease fix,
and despite the clock ticking down on their high school experience, this
was West Hartford, there was nothing to do, and they were bored. So
Dylan floated out "one more week" to no one in particular on this hot
June day, just trying to sound philosophical.

Noah bit. "Speaking of which, did you sign my yearbook yet?"

"I'll bring them all tonight," Dylan promised. "Did you losers sign
mine yet?"

From the back seat, Walker Schlossberg piped up. "I know what I'm
going to write. Noah's the logjam." It was true that Jew-fro'd Walker
knew exactly what he was going to write in everyone's yearbook. He'd

been working on his messages for months. He'd narrowed down their years of shared experiences to only the most significant events, those handful of turning points that would truly spell out how he felt about his friends. Then he planned on adding a sprinkle of small, obscure anecdotes—like the time Dylan stole the *Red Asphalt* DVD from Driver's Ed and switched it with their health class movie on menstruation. So the fact that Noah still had Dylan's yearbook and Dylan had everyone else's was actually kind of frustrating to Walker.

But Walker was used to being frustrated. The only virgin among the four friends, Walker, despite his name, was a doormat. He liked to say he just really respected women, but the other three guys knew that seventeen-year-old girls weren't looking for respect. They were looking for someone to tip the scales of their precarious self-esteem by making them feel special. In other words, they were looking for someone who wasn't a complete pussy.

The yearbook had come out two weeks ago and it was actually a big deal at Hall High School. Maybe it was because most of the seniors had known each other since elementary school. Or maybe it was because in New England, there were so many colleges that the graduates fanned out across the region, and even close friends rarely attended the same school. Whatever the reason, yearbooks were serious business. People had signing parties, reserved whole pages for their best friends, and really thought about what they were going to say. After all, it was an emotional time in their lives and even the manliest among them bared their souls on those pages.

Still, Dylan wasn't above giving Noah shit for hogging his yearbook. "Dude, it doesn't count towards your GPA. You going to make a photo collage, too?"

"Hey, excuse me if it takes a while to summarize eighteen years of being friends with you, asshole," Noah shot back. If trading insults was the way guys show affection, these four were madly in love with each other.

The truth was, Noah was stuck. Maybe Walker was planning on wowing the others with his total recall of events both profound and obscure, but Noah simply wanted to tell Dylan how he really felt. How he was going to miss him next year as they went off their separate ways. How much he appreciated Dylan being there for him through the pain and heartache of high school. But Noah wasn't a poet, and he couldn't even figure out how to begin.

Jeff Pike spoke. "One more week of high school and we're still sitting here in the McDonald's parking lot like a bunch of douches." The skinny stoner with short blond hair and an even shorter fuse took a drag off the remnants of the joint he was smoking. Whereas Dylan had outgrown pot in like eighth grade, Noah never really got a buzz off it, and Walker was afraid to even try it, Pike was a true believer in the power of the bud. That's why Pike alone among them ran in two crowds: his life-long friends who tolerated the smoke and the stink and the stupid things he said when he was stoned; and his stoner friends, with whom he actually got high.

Dylan shifted his weight restlessly. "Pike's right. Let's do something."

"How about Friendly's?" Walker suggested, just trying to be helpful.

No reaction.

"We can go hang out at Sarah's pool…" Noah offered, but the other three quickly quashed that idea with a simultaneous, "No!"

Pike took another hit. Walker waved the smoke away from his face with an effeminate swish. Noah scrounged for any stray bonus fries at the bottom of the grease-stained bag.

As usual, it fell on Dylan to come up with the real plan. "I know. How about a High Speed Test?"

"Sure. Why not?" Noah seconded. "Mountain Road?"

"Seventy-two," Dylan reminded him.

"Fern?" Walker offered.

"Seventy-five."

Noah consulted the Google Map in his mind. "How about Brookline?"

"Ooh, good choice," Dylan affirmed. He put the Cube in gear and pulled out of the parking lot onto North Main Street.

The premise of the High Speed Test was simple: How fast could Dylan drive on a particular residential street without killing himself, his passengers, or random pedestrians. Some of these speeds were frighteningly high, especially given the condition of the roads after the snow plows had had their way with them all winter long.

After a mile and a right turn, they arrived at Brookline, a tree-lined lane with a posted speed limit of twenty-five. It was a quiet road that didn't lead anywhere important, so it received little traffic besides the four-wheel-drive Subarus that parked in the driveways. Inside the large colonial houses, with their muted colors of aluminum siding, lived an aging population mixed with a few younger families. And unfortunately for Brookline, the road was stick straight and practically begged for drag racing.

Dylan stopped the car at the end of the street and queued up the

Eels' "Mr. E's Beautiful Blue." Satisfied with his selection, he turned to the other three. "Ready?"

Walker checked his seatbelt. Noah rolled up the bag of McDonald's and stowed it under the seat. Pike took a last drag off the joint and pinched it out. He rolled up his window.

"Hit it," Pike ordered.

Dylan stepped on the gas. They accelerated quickly, and in no time they were doing fifty down this sleepy lane.

Noah read off the speedometer, as Dylan was going too fast to even glance down. "Sixty... sixty-five... seventy."

They were going crazy fast for this street and Walker, as usual, was the first to crack. "Okay, slow down. Slow down, Dylan!"

But it wasn't a "medium speed test," and Dylan had no intention of braking. Noah kept his eyes glued to the speedometer. Pike started laughing his ass off, feeding off the adrenaline. Walker gripped his seat with white knuckles. But Dylan was confident, feeling invulnerable, focused only on the road.

"Eighty..." Noah counted off.

Then Walker screamed, "Look out!"

Up ahead, an old man on a riding lawnmower was in the *middle of the street*, making a U-turn back toward his house.

Dylan swerved, and before anyone's brain had time to process what was happening, the Cube jumped the curb and drove right across the guy's front lawn, passing the lawnmower at more than three times the speed limit.

In an instant, they were on the next block, with the stunned John Deere driver way behind them, shaking his fist at the guys like a cartoon old coot.

Dylan overcorrected and slammed on the brakes. Unfortunately, that only made the Cube spin out of control. As opposed to the previous maneuver, which felt like it was over in a flash, spinning 360 degrees in the middle of Brookline seemed to last forever. As if in slow motion, Dylan looked over and saw Noah staring back at him calmly, like, *It's been a pleasure serving with you.* He glanced in the rear-view mirror and saw Walker with his eyes closed, seemingly accepting his certain death. Then, as the car continued to spin into its second rotation, Dylan spotted Pike smiling ear to ear. This was the most fun he'd had in ages.

Finally, the Cube came to a complete stop right in the middle of the street and stalled out.

The guys were frozen in shock. They sat there for a moment, stunned, until their hearts started beating again. Miraculously, they were still alive and the car hadn't hit anything.

Noah finally broke the silence: "Brookline. Eighty-one."

They all burst out laughing.

Without another word on the subject, Dylan simply turned the ignition back on and drove off.

CHAPTER TWO

THAT EVENING, DYLAN sat in his bedroom listening to Keane on his iPod and finishing his yearbook entries as promised. Aside from a few dusty soccer trophies and a photo of his mom, Dylan's room was surprisingly undecorated. No *Star Wars* sheets or Clash posters here. Dylan was never much of a collector in the first place, but the simple white sheets and bare walls made it hard to believe that a teenager lived there. It was almost as if Dylan had considered his room temporary lodging for the last eighteen years.

He was almost done signing the yearbooks—he'd written most of the messages yesterday in study hall—but he wanted to go over them one more time just to make sure he was setting the right tone. These were his best friends, after all, not some random acquaintance like portly Stu Wexley, whose yearbook Dylan signed in the hallway between periods with three lines about (1) playing soccer together in sixth grade, (2) the time Stu ate fifteen chicken cutlet sandwiches in the cafeteria on a bet (and later puked up his guts), and (3) the retarded substitute teacher they'd had one day in Spanish class who fell for the old "Mike Hawk" gag during roll call.

Dylan picked up Noah's yearbook first and started skimming through it, stopping at a picture of Noah with Sarah at the Halloween Dance. They'd gone as Wall-e and Eve and they looked happy. But by the Valentine's Day Dance (two pages later), you could tell they were losing that loving feeling. And anyone who'd witnessed the fight they had at Prom (too recent to make it into the yearbook) would have had a hard time explaining why they were still together. Now, Dylan didn't mind his friends' girlfriends messing up the guy dynamic, but if Sarah was just going to yell and cry and pout all the time, he felt that it was his duty as Noah's best friend to push him in the direction of dumping the bitch.

Dylan had written on the page Noah saved for him on the inside cover (the most prestigious real estate in the yearbook):

Noah—
Where to begin? We've been friends since kindergarten, when you were putting dolls in the pretend oven and making the girls scream. That's when I thought, this kid's pretty cool.
Alot of funny shit has happened over the years. Mr. Swanson catching us ditching class to go see Batman Begins. Monica Krasnitz's bat mitzvah (remember her cousin Jennifer? Told you she'd let you get to third base!). And don't forget about that ski trip junior year. Dude, NEVER ski drunk!!!
So many memories it's hard to pick the ones to write about. But every time I think about something big in my life, you were right there with me. First time I got drunk? Your

Dad's Johnny Walker Red. First time I got laid? Okay, maybe you weren't there, but you were the first one I told. You are such a big part of my life, it's hard to imagine how I could have made it through high school without you. You're like a brother to me and I'm really gonna miss you next year.

I hope things work out with Sarah, but if they don't, just remember that you're a smart guy—probably the smartest guy I know—and you'll find what you're looking for if you look hard enough.

Your friend,
Dylan

Dylan corrected a couple of mistakes ("'a lot' is two words," he remembered Mr. Travoli harping on him), then put Noah's yearbook aside and turned to Walker's.

If Noah was Dylan's wingman, Walker was more like the little brother Dylan never had. After all, Walker was alternately clueless and pathetic, and it was hard not to assume a superior attitude to someone who let so many opportunities to score slip through his fingers. Accordingly, Dylan had signed Walker's yearbook with a bit of a pep talk:

Walker—
You're a great guy, man, and pretty soon girls are going to pick up on that. Trust me, you are going to get laid like crazy in college. I just think you're the kind of guy who girls appreciate when they're older.

At least Dylan hoped so. After all, this was the same Walker who spent nine months secretly pursuing a cute girl from his chemistry class, consoled her for an entire weekend when she found out her boyfriend was cheating on her, then stood by while she forgave the scumbag and lost her virginity to him the next weekend!

I think you just need a little more confidence. Like that time you stood up to Marc Jenner. You didn't think you had it in you, but boom! One punch in the nose and the pussy starts crying like a little bitch.

I'm not saying you need to punch girls.

That's as far as Dylan had gotten signing Walker's yearbook. He decided to scratch out the last line and continued writing:

Look, man, I don't want to lecture you. I just want you to know that you're a fucking cool dude and as soon as you realize that, so will everyone else. I'm gonna miss your sense of humor and all the funny shit you say.

You are going to have a great life.

—Dylan

Dylan put Walker's yearbook aside and turned up the volume on his iPod. It was the Breeders' "Cannonball," and he had a soft spot in his heart for female alt rock from before he was born. He flipped open Pike's yearbook and reread what he had written:

Pike—

From the first time I met you and you were doing whippets

in the back of home ec class, I knew you were one crazy motherfucker—

Pike wasn't the kind of guy you got mushy about, but you could always count on him for something outrageous, like the time Dylan found him in his parents' basement naked, playing *Call of Duty* with a bong rigged to a snorkel. Or his Ninja phase, where Pike carried a pair of nunchucks wherever he went (that particular affectation ended suddenly when one day Pike literally knocked himself out).

I could always count on you to make shit fun. You really know how to live in the moment and I love that about you.

I think you're gonna have a sweet time out in Calif. next year. Sounds like the perfect place for you.

It's funny. Part of me wonders what "college Pike" will be like. Are you going to be "that" guy with the weed and the bong collection or are you going to reinvent yourself somehow? Don't want to sound like a dick here, but I bet Pike 20 is even more awesome than the pot-smoking Pike I know.

Anyway, I know whenever the shit hit the fan (as it usually did), you always had my back. You're a good friend and I'm gonna miss the shit out of you, man.

—Dylan

Dylan continued flipping, reading what classmates had written under their pictures, trying to figure out the coded phrases and inside jokes. Then he saw a picture of the four of them freshman year—just a candid photo hanging out in back of the school by the soccer field. He couldn't believe how young they all looked!

Suddenly, Dylan swelled with emotion. It came on without warning and the intensity surprised him. Something was really messing with his head and he found himself actually fighting back a tear.

Oh, my God, what a pussy, Dylan's left brain told his right.

Then, "Dylan!" came a booming voice from the hallway.

Dylan closed the yearbook, hoping that would shut out those unwanted emotions. He took out his earphones, preparing for the inevitable confrontation. Soon, Dylan's blue-collar dad appeared in the doorway with an envelope in his hand.

Dylan's dad was forty-two, still pretty young, relatively speaking (he'd had Dylan when he was twenty-four). He had a goatee, a full head of dark hair, and the body of someone who worked for a living. Not chiseled, but strong.

And handsome. Still, Dylan's dad never remarried after Dylan's mom died, unless you count his paving company. He'd built Glasco Paving into one of the most successful paving companies in the state, and he didn't do it by taking a lot of time off. "You want something in life, you work for it," was one of his favorite sayings, along with the equally folksy, "If a job's worth doing, it's worth doing right." Not surprisingly, all of his little aphorisms were about work. He didn't have any pithy truisms about spending time with your son or actually getting to know the other person who lives in your house.

"Dylan, what is this?" he demanded, waving the envelope like Exhibit A.

"Why are you opening my mail?" Dylan deflected.

"Goddamn it, we agreed, you're going to college!" His dad was turning red.

"No, *you* did! I'm eighteen. I can do what I want."

"Not while you're living under my roof!"

Wow, Dylan couldn't believe he resorted to that oldie but goodie. Dylan got up off the bed and grabbed the three yearbooks. "Well, that's not for much longer."

"Where do you think you're going?"

"Out." He brushed past his dad, avoiding eye contact.

"Dylan!"

Dylan could tell his dad was pleading now. Dylan rolled his eyes, stopped, and turned back to face him.

His dad took a deep breath. "I worked my butt off so you could have the opportunities I didn't have."

This was him trying to relate, Dylan figured. But Dylan wasn't in the mood for a tender family moment. The time for that was eleven years ago. Maybe if his dad had poured his energy into his family after the car accident, instead of work, things would have been different. Maybe then his dad wouldn't seem like a stranger to him. But it was too little too late now.

"Are we done?" Dylan asked rhetorically. He didn't wait for an answer.

CHAPTER THREE

SOON, DYLAN WAS back with his friends, parked in the Walgreens lot across the street from a "package store," Connecticut parlance for liquor store. The guys were now dressed for an evening out, which meant jeans and a tight white v-neck t-shirt for Dylan, jeans and a striped polo shirt for Noah, khakis and button-down for Walker, and a tie-dye, cargo shorts, and flip flops for Pike. The guys sat in anxious silence for a while with the engine off, windows open, and headlights on. They were waiting for something, and their patience was wearing thin.

"What the fuck is taking so long?" Pike asked, annoyed.

Walker ventured a guess. "Maybe that guy was schizophrenic or something."

"Yeah, or maybe he's manning the glory hole around back," Noah offered with a snicker.

Once again, it was Dylan's job to rally the troops. "Relax, there he is."

And there, across the street, staggering out of the liquor store, was a homeless guy. Not the most disgusting homeless guy you ever saw, but pretty close. He was white, at least under the topsoil, with matted hair and clothes that smelled like old shellfish and pee. He glanced over at the Cube, and spotting his partners in crime, waved at the guys.

"Subtle," Noah commented.

The homeless guy waited for a moment, looking at them for a signal. Then, he motioned, like, *Should I come to you?*

Pike answered, though the guy clearly couldn't hear him. "Yes, fucknut. Cross the street. Walk like an Egyptian."

The homeless guy started crossing the street. By now, the guys could see he was carrying a brown paper bag, the kind you might associate with a wino. Walker was the first to pick up on it. "Anyone notice something missing?" And Pike was the first to go apeshit about it. "Oh, for fuck's sake. He didn't get it."

Dylan heaved a big sigh. "I'll take care of this." He got out of the car and after a quick round of *Should we wait here?* looks, the other three followed suit.

Dylan stood in front of his car and waited for the homeless guy to reach him. (No way Dylan was setting foot in the package store parking lot.) When the guy finally stumbled up to him, Dylan forced a smile like they were old friends. "Hey, man. What happened? Where's the beer?"

The homeless guy thought about it for a second then replied, "They were all out?" In actuality, the words were halfway between a statement and a question. Clearly this dude had a lot bigger fish to fry than trying to lie convincingly. The guys looked at each other, confused.

"You were supposed to buy a case of MGD," Dylan reminded him, holding back his anger. "What's in the bag?"

The homeless guy held up the wino sack with its mystery contents.

"This is much better. Good for you," he pitched.

Pike swiped the bag and pulled out a bottle of low-grade, candy-flavored swill. "What the fuck?! We can't bring this!" he yelled.

Noah couldn't help but laugh at the absurd liquor choice.

Then the ever-observant Walker noticed something else. "Uh, guys… It's open."

Now even Dylan was pissed. He took a step closer to the guy, escalating the threat level. "Did you drink some of this?" he accused.

The homeless guy threw up his hands. "Shit, Grissom, you got me. I thought we was in this together."

Dylan rubbed his brow. This had turned into a disaster. Ask a homeless guy to buy you beer and you expect a prompt and courteous transaction. But what's the point of arguing now, when the deal's already been fucked up beyond repair? Dylan tried to cut his losses. "Just give me the change."

But for some reason, this really set the guy off. "You said I could keep it!"

Pike stepped in. "Yeah, if you bought us a case of beer! Not a liter of fucking Boone's Farms Mixed Berry Schnapps!"

The homeless guy shook his head. He tried to offer these kids the benefit of his years of experience, explaining, "This shit will get you fucked *up*!"

Noah checked the time on his iPhone. "Let's just go."

The guys turned to leave, willing to chalk this up to "you win some, you lose some." But the homeless guy's eyes were still glued to that bottle in Pike's hand.

"I ain't done with it!" The guy made his move, darting toward Pike with a seemingly impossible burst of speed, swiping the bottle back.

Pike furrowed his brow in an *oh, no you didn't* look and easily repossessed it. They locked eyes and struggled over the bottle for a second. But then, as if in slow motion, the bottle slipped from their hands and smashed on the ground.

The homeless guy was incensed. "You dick!"

And with that, he reached into the back of his pants and pulled out... a log.

That's right. Actual shit.

The guys' eyes went wide.

"Watch out!" Dylan shouted.

"He's got a doodie!" Noah screamed.

The guys scrambled for the car as the insane hobo *whipped his shit at them*. The four of them dodged the projectile like their lives depended on it (thank you, Gym Teacher Murphy) and the log hit the windshield of Dylan's car with a tremendous SPLATTT!!!

The guys jumped into the car and slammed the doors shut.

Pike saw the guy reaching again. "He's got another one!"

"Where's he getting all this shit?!" Walker screamed.

Noah yelled back, "He's probably been saving it up for weeks!"

Dylan started the ignition. "Let's get out of here!"

SPLATTT!!! Another literal shit bomb hit the car and some fragments went through the open windows.

Pike screamed. "I think some went in my mouth!"

The guys frantically tried to close the windows, but power windows only go up so fast. "Hurry! Hurry!" Walker pleaded.

The windows finally sealed shut, and Dylan peeled out just as another log hit the rear window.

CHAPTER FOUR

FIFTEEN MINUTES AND eight quarters later, the windshield wipers smeared the poop across the glass as the all-night car-wash jets attempted to dilute the brown stain. Inside the Cube, the guys watched the turds wash away to the inappropriately mellow Iron and Wine song, "Belated Promise Ring." Pike took a big swig of red Gatorade and started gargling with it. He opened the door a crack and spit it onto the pavement. Pike shuddered. "He probably has AIDS."

Walker reassured him. "You can't get AIDS from eating someone's poop."

But Pike was in no mood to be placated. "Well, you can get fucking hepatitis! Or— or— fucking... who knows what's in that guy's shit!"

"Other... Men's... Sperm..." Noah reminded him with a self-satisfied chuckle.

In a few moments, the guys could see out of the front windshield again. But they were still short a case of beer and time was running out.

Walker looked at Dylan for guidance. "So now what? Find another homeless guy?"

Dylan pointed to the clock on the dash. "We're screwed."

Sure enough, the clock read 9:04.

Pike, still in a foul mood, launched into another tirade. "God, I fucking hate Connecticut! No other state in the nation closes the liquor stores at fucking nine p.m."

"They do in the South," Walker corrected.

"Well, they don't in Massachusetts," Pike countered.

Before that idea could take hold, Dylan shut it down. "We're not driving to Massachusetts."

Noah looked defeated. "So, what, we just go home?"

But Dylan wasn't giving up on the evening just yet. "No, let me talk to Marco." He turned on the ignition.

When they arrived at the sprawling Tudor at 7 Westmore Lane, there was already a line of people trying to get into Marco's house. And what's more, they were all carrying some kind of alcohol, whether a case of beer, a liter of vodka, or even a bottle of champagne. At the door wasn't Marco Rosenbaum himself, of course—Marco was far too busy to play bouncer at his own party. Nope, it was Chuck Zambrelli, a big, hulking member of the football team. Not smart, quick, or agile enough to be the quarterback, running back, or receiver, Chuck was one of the human blocking dummies that made up the offensive line. And tonight he was taking liquor bottles for entry, as was the custom at Marco's.

The guys waited in line anxiously until they finally got up to the front door.

"S'up, ladies," Chuck bellowed, making himself laugh.

Dylan stepped forward. "Look, man. We had a case of MGD lined up, but there was a mix up. Long story short, we don't have anything.

Can we give you cash this time?"

"Yeah, that's gonna be a problem." Chuck was not mentally equipped to deviate from his specific instructions.

It looked like an impasse. Three lacrosse players behind the guys held up a bottle of Stoli and Chuck grabbed it from over Dylan's head. He waved them through and they squeezed by the guys to get into the party. A quartet of sophomore girls struggled to pass a case of Smirnoff Ice to Chuck. Dylan moved over slightly to let them get by, too.

Chuck looked at Dylan, who clearly wasn't going away. Chuck had to do something. These four losers looked pathetic and were blocking the flow of traffic. Chuck rolled his eyes and said, "All right, you little bitches, just wait here." Then something wafted into his nostrils. Chuck sniffed the air for a second. Did someone poop their pants? Chuck closed the door on them.

As the guys waited, Dylan turned to Noah and brought up a sensitive subject. "So. You going to talk to Sarah?"

Noah was defensive. "Why do you care so much about me and Sarah?"

"I *don't* care. *You're* the one who keeps whining about her. I'm just saying, get it over with. Make a clean break. It's gonna hurt a lot more later."

Pike seconded the motion, "Rip that pus-filled band-aid off!"

Noah relented under the peer pressure. "All right, shut up already, I'll talk to her."

Only Walker was thinking ahead. "If you guys break up, do you think she'll go out with me?"

Noah just glared at him.

Then the door opened once again. It was Marco Rosenbaum, in the flesh. Marco looked like a young Donald Trump—he even had the hair. And who wears a tie to a high school party? But Marco thought of himself as less of a host or a guy whose parents go out of town a lot, and more like a concierge. It was his job to provide entertainment and meet the needs of fun-starved high school kids.

West Hartford didn't have all-ages clubs or trendy late-night bookstores or open-air promenades for teenagers to hang out in. And Hartford, the insurance capital of the country, wasn't much better. So the desperate students of Hall High School were forced to make their own fun at whosever house was available, and that usually meant Marco's. All Marco asked in return was liquor. Or drugs.

"Hey, guys. What happened?" Marco asked with a note of fake concern.

"It's a long story…" Dylan started.

But Pike gave the executive summary: "Some homeless dude bought us mixed berry schnapps but he went mental and threw his poop at us."

Marco folded his arms and with one hand stroked his nonexistent beard thoughtfully. "Hmm, fascinating. Have you lined up any publishers for that story?"

Dylan pleaded. "Can we pay you cash instead?"

Marco smiled. "Guys. Come on. Are you new in town? Did your dad just get transferred in from Worcester?"

Noah saw Dylan was out of ammo and like a good wingman came in guns blazing. "Come on, Marco. We've probably bought you ten grand worth of booze over the years. We're graduating next week. Cut us some slack."

Marco was not the type to be persuaded by such sob stories. "Sure, no problem. Maybe I can get you a warm compress and massage your balls while we're at it."

Then, in a last-ditch effort, Dylan tried to appeal to his humanity. "Dude, it's Saturday night in West Hartford. Where else are we going to go?"

Marco thought it over. Not so much because he felt like being nice, but more so because they guys were holding up the line and time was money, Marco relented.

"Fine. Twenty bucks. And you bring double to Beach Weekend."

Marco was of course referring the party of the year taking place next weekend at his parents' beach house in Rhode Island. Graduation was the following Wednesday, so Beach Weekend was the last party of high school. All the seniors went, as it was *the* unofficial send-off every year.

But that was next weekend and this was this weekend. Marco was letting them into the party without the entry booze and Dylan sighed a breath of relief. "Thanks," he said as he pulled out a twenty.

Marco smirked ever so slightly. "Each."

The guys rolled their eyes, but they knew they had no choice. They all pulled out their wallets and paid twenty bucks to get into Marco's house.

CHAPTER FIVE

THE FOUR GUYS descended the staircase into Club Rosenbaum, what in the 70s they might have called a "rec room." There was a ping pong table (with no net), lots of old couches and ripped beanbag chairs, neon beer signs, and a large wood-paneled bar. It smelled like stale beer from the years of spills onto the thin grey carpet. Dozens of teenagers lounged around with beers and mixed drinks while Marco's Party Playlist #44 was pumped through the stereo (current selection: "Kelly Watch the Stars" by AIR). A large number of the kids were signing yearbooks. All in all, it was pretty unimpressive, but in high school you take what you can get.

Ned, an odd-looking stoner dude with weird buck teeth and a feathered fedora, came up to Pike. "What uuuuuuuuppppp?" The two did a handshake/hug combo. Ned was the guy in high school whose brain was so fried that he was fun to have around because no matter what, he made you look good. Plus, Ned always had weed.

"Shake and bake?" Pike asked rhetorically.

"Fire it up," Ned replied. The two of them went off to Marco's Dad's work room, leaving Dylan, Noah, and Walker to fend for themselves.

"Come on, let's grab a beer," Dylan suggested. "I'm getting my twenty bucks worth." The three of them went over to the bar area and grabbed some beers from the refrigerator. Ironically, they happened to be Miller Genuine Drafts.

Noah looked around. Even for West Hartford, Club Rosenbaum was pretty sad and pathetic. "Gonna be hard giving all this up next year," Noah said facetiously. He ripped a loose swatch of faux leather off the ancient barstool. A big football player at the end of the bar did a flaming shot to the delight of his teammates.

To Noah's surprise, Dylan was nostalgic. "You say that now, but trust me, you're going to look back fondly on these days."

Walker felt the same way. He raised his bottle and toasted, "Here's to the Class of 2012." They clinked bottles and drank.

Just then, Lisa, a cute, short girl with curly brown hair, came up to Noah with her yearbook. "Hey, Noah, can you sign mine?"

"Sure," Noah replied. He took her yearbook over to the ping pong table to sign it.

It was weird. After eighteen years of friendships, rivalries, after-school fist fights, and random hook-ups, in the end, the extraneous feelings all sort of washed away and left only camaraderie. Like, *We're all in this together*. And it showed in times like these as the final days of high school ticked down, when everyone signed everyone else's yearbook without dwelling on the bad stuff. Maybe sometimes you had to dig deep to remember playing on the same little league team with Lucas Westerly, now a totally tatted-up gearhead. Or the time you skipped school with Tom Weaver in eighth grade to go see *Superbad*, before you two drifted apart. But no matter how tenuous or antagonistic the relationship was in the past, practically no one refused to sign a yearbook, if asked. And no one betrayed that trust by writing something mean.

Back at the bar, Dylan saw Walker staring across the room at a cute girl. Walker noticed Dylan eyeing him and asked, "Who's *that*?"

"Don't know," Dylan admitted. "But she is hot as hell."

Walker was salivating.

"Go talk to her," Dylan suggested, though he knew that was about as likely as asking him to go pet a velociraptor.

"Yeah, right," Walker scoffed predictably.

Dylan rolled his eyes, then, without warning, put two fingers in his mouth and whistled. The girl looked up and Dylan confidently motioned for her to come over to them... which she did!

Walker had good taste. This girl was gorgeous and had a kind of aristocratic look about her, with long, straight, dark hair that contrasted against her alabaster skin. She clearly didn't go to Hall with them or Dylan would have bedded her years ago. She arrived at the bar with a big smile, curious and thankful to be noticed.

"Strange girl we've never seen before," Dylan ad libbed, "this is Walker. 3.7 GPA, going to Brandeis next year, super sexy. He'd like to get to know you."

Walker's heart was racing. His instincts were telling him to get the hell out of there, but he fought them back and forced an uncomfortable smile. Then, to his surprise, this girl actually blushed a little. "Okay," she said.

Walker couldn't believe that just worked. "Sorry about him," he said, uncharacteristically seizing the moment. "Hi, I'm Walker."

"Patience," she replied. Walker hoped it was her name and not some sort of cryptic message. He shook her hand.

"You want to get a beer?" he suggested and Patience nodded. Walker escorted her to the refrigerator, leaving Dylan alone.

But not for long. A random guy Dylan thought he might have had Algebra II with approached with a yearbook.

"Dylan! Sign my yearbook, dude."

Dylan took it, confident he could piece together something to write by reading what everyone else had written in this guy's yearbook.

Meanwhile, at the ping pong table, Noah finished signing Lisa's yearbook and handed it back to her. Suddenly, a hand slid in from behind Noah's back and covered his eyes. This person was clearly a girl, but she tried to use her best fake deep voice, asking gruffly, "Guess who?"

With her hand still over his eyes, Noah turned around and kissed her before guessing, "Mike?"

She lowered her hand and Noah pretended to be surprised at seeing his girlfriend. "Oh, my God. Sarah. I've said too much."

Sarah laughed along with his lame ruse. Sarah was a pretty girl with wavy blonde hair and a curvy body to match. She had big breasts and liked to wear tight tank tops that made them look even bigger. Not that Noah ever complained. It had been nine months since they got together, almost their entire senior year, and for a teenager that was an eternity. Noah first hooked up with Sarah at Scott Wheeler's house right after the Jewish holidays. Then they just kept hooking up with each other and no one else, when one day in October, Sarah changed her Facebook status to "In a Relationship."

Things were great—better than great—for a long time. But it was hard work maintaining a serious relationship for their entire senior year of high school. There were all sorts of temptations to hook up with other people that Noah and Sarah had successfully avoided. But there were also a million other things pulling them in different directions, from friends to extra-curricular activities to college applications. Lately, there was also a growing restlessness that they both felt, a need to prepare for the future in which they were free to explore the world on their own. And, of course, there was graduation itself, a bright-line, fatal cut-off date marching ever closer.

In high school, you think that every relationship is the one. Not counting random or even repeat hook-ups, of course. But when things turn serious, both parties assume it's love and destiny and God smiling on them. Sarah certainly felt this way. And so did Noah. Until it stopped being fun. But Noah didn't have the benefit of years of relationship experience to know whether this truly was a doomed relationship or just growing pains that all couples have to work through. Who's to say they weren't supposed to figure out how to make it all work and live happily ever after? It didn't sound so crazy after all. The truth was Noah just wasn't sure.

But Dylan had been hounding him for months to break up with Sarah. True, Dylan didn't believe in relationships in the first place, but he was persuasive when he said, "If it's not fun anymore, what's the point?" Noah had been broaching the subject with Sarah for weeks by delicately asking what they were going to do after graduation. But deep down, Noah didn't want Sarah to be like those karate classes he took at the Y in third grade, where he just gave up after it got too hard. Maybe he was supposed to be a black belt today and he changed the cosmic timeline by quitting too easily.

So when Noah turned to Sarah and said, "Hey, babe. One more week," it was an immediate downer.

Sarah's smile faded and she just muttered, "Yeah."

Suddenly, it was awkward. Avoiding eye contact, Noah asked, "So are we going to talk about this?" He glanced over and saw Dylan giving him a look of moral support.

Sarah put on her game face and took Noah's hand with a smile. "Do we have to do this now? It's a party."

"If you call it that," Noah replied. "Look, I just think we need to figure things out before graduation."

Maybe Sarah was in complete denial about their impending doom. Or maybe she just wanted to avoid the heartache for as long as possible. Whatever the reason, Sarah pulled out her trump card and said, "Not now. I'm horny." She knew no guy was going to say no to that, and she smiled seductively as she led him toward the stairs. Maybe she had only delayed the conversation for another day or two, but for now Sarah was pleased with herself, and inside she was gloating about the power girls had over guys.

As he ascended the stairway to heaven, Noah locked eyes with a visibly disappointed Dylan. Noah's look said, *What can I do? I tried.*

Dylan just shook his head. What a chicken-shit.

With Walker chatting up Patience on the couch, Noah off with Sarah, and Pike in a cloud of smoke in the work room, Dylan was alone now. He swigged the last of his beer and left the empty on the bar. A cute sophomore girl was walking toward him. She looked young and had an insecure vibe about her, as if she was overly self-conscious about even being at a senior party. Dylan was sure he'd seen her in the cafeteria before, but there were a lot of cute girls at Hall High and Dylan couldn't keep track of all of them. As she was about to pass him, Dylan stopped her without missing a beat.

"Whoa, whoa, whoa," Dylan said, pointing to her chest and sounding serious. "You've got 'updoc' all over your shirt."

The cute girl took the bait. "What's 'updoc'?"

Dylan put his finger to his mouth and did his best Elmer Fudd: "Shhh! Be vewy, vewy qwiet. I'm hunting wabbits."

She actually laughed at this, as Dylan had no doubt that she would. He grinned, with a smile that was time-tested and well-honed for perceived sincerity. "Hi, I'm Dylan," was all he needed to say to seal the deal. Looks like all those years of watching old cartoons really paid off.

―――――

Back on the couch, Walker was making headway of his own. Patience really seemed into him. You could tell by her body language, the way she leaned in to face him, laughed at his lame attempts at jokes, and even touched his arm. Unfortunately, Walker failed to notice any of this.

"I'm visiting my friend Tracy," Patience explained. "I go to Choate. Well, I used to. God, it's so weird to think we already graduated."

She leaned forward and Walker tried his hardest not to look down her shirt. After all, his strategy was to appeal to her mind, not insult her with base leering. "Where are you going next year?" he asked.

"Wellesley."

Walker saw his in. "Wow, I'm going to be in Boston. Well, just outside. Brandeis. We should exchange emails."

Patience smiled. Tragically, Walker thought things were going great. Like maybe after he got her email, they could become Facebook friends.

Then, after they got to know each other over the summer, he'd arrange a meeting in Boston in the Fall once they were settled in. A dinner date, maybe a movie, and before you know it, they'd have that magic first kiss.

Unbeknownst to him, Patience was growing bored. She had been giving him the signal from the moment they met that she was looking for a meaningless hook-up, but this guy kept talking and talking. *Ugh, what does a girl have to do to get laid these days?*, she thought behind that smile.

Next door, in the concrete-floored work room, the stoners were sitting on a ratty old plaid couch passing a bong. The stoner crowd was usually a mix-and-match group of potheads with an occasional "respectable" teen getting high on a lark. Today it was just the core group: Pike, Ned, Suzanne, Olaf, and Diaz.

Suzanne was kind of cute, with scraggly strawberry blonde hair and freckles. You might hook up with her if you were high, and since everyone here usually was, everyone here had.

Olaf was a foreign exchange student from Norway and immediately befriended the group. Back home, practically any gorgeous Norwegian girl would have sex with you just to be polite, but smoking pot, it seemed, was still kind of a taboo. (This confused Ned for the first several weeks after meeting Olaf, because Ned mixed up Norway and The Netherlands.) So, naturally, when Olaf came to the U.S. for the year, he wasn't as interested in hooking up as he was in getting baked. And he took it as a personal challenge to become the best at it. Which he was.

Whereas Olaf was welcomed with open arms by the other stoners, and frequently provided some of the most hilarious lines when stoned (like the time he said, "Ja man, this bud is sweeter than my mother's teet."), Diaz, on the other hand, just kind of latched onto the group without any invitation, formal or otherwise. Truth be told, no one really liked Diaz. He never said anything funny or worthwhile, he mooched off of everyone else and never provided his own weed, and frankly he kind of smelled. Like cheese. Furthermore, he looked like a troll. Pike saw him in the boys' locker room shower one day and swore he had a tail. But stoners aren't haters and unlike their violent, aggressive counterparts in the world of teenage binge drinking, everyone was welcome to partake in a bong hit. Even a troll.

Pike took a hit and passed the bong to Suzanne. As he held in the smoke, Pike stared at the work bench with its rotary saw. He exhaled, then slowly looked over at the power tools hanging on a peg board above the work bench. As if a powerful revelation had come to him, he asked the group, "Did you ever really look at all these tools?"

Ned repeated, "Tools," and guffawed.

But Pike felt like he had hit upon something here. Maybe something important. "No, seriously. I mean, like, think about it. One day some guy just said, 'I'm going to invent like a *drill*.'"

The five of them thought about it for a second, then burst out laughing like it was the funniest thing they'd ever heard.

———————————

In Marco's parents' bedroom, Sarah and Noah were making out like crazy. Noah often wondered where Marco's parents went all the time. Marco's dad was rich and Marco's 29-year-old step-mom had just had his half-brother, Jaden. They must take the baby with them on vacation or something. He didn't spend *too* much time thinking about it though, because at the end of the day he didn't really care. Still, he wondered if he and Sarah had more sex in this bed than Marco's parents.

In between kisses, Sarah told Noah, "I've been waiting for this all week. I am so stressed out over finals."

"Why do you care?" Noah reassured her. "Wisconsin isn't even going to look at these grades."

"I don't want to talk about it," Sarah replied.

You brought it up, Noah thought, but then Sarah whipped off her shirt and jeans and hopped on the bed, erasing all prior thoughts from his mind. Sarah did the seductive "come here" finger.

Noah smiled. This was what was so great about having a real girlfriend. No mind games and no mystery, like, *Am I going to get lucky or not?* Noah knew he was going to have sex and that certainty was comforting to him. He took off his shirt and pulled out a condom before peeling off his pants. On the way over to the bed he turned off the lights.

Noah kissed Sarah with fiery intensity. Then he started kissing her neck while he cradled her head in one hand and expertly undid her bra with the other. Again, an advantage of having a real girlfriend: Noah knew her bra clasps by heart.

Sarah was really getting into it and Noah could tell by her little moans that his kisses were having the desired effect. Time to shift into second gear. He travelled little kisses down to her breasts on his usual flight plan, and his hand moved down to explore under her panties. Her little gasps and moans grew louder and quicker. She reached into his boxer briefs and pulled out his dick. Now it was Noah who was starting to moan.

This went on for a moment or two before Sarah couldn't take it anymore. "I want you. Now."

You didn't have to tell Noah twice. "Yes, ma'am," he replied.

Noah reached over to the condom and opened it up. He fumbled around with it for a moment. Sarah waited patiently. But this was taking a little too long. Noah was having some technical difficulties getting the condom on. Then, *snap*! Noah screamed!

Sarah sat up. "What's wrong?"

"Condom broke."

Click. Sarah turned on the night table lamp. Noah examined the condom, trying to figure out if he could salvage it. He wasn't sure if it was a manufacturing defect or if it had gotten pierced by something in his pocket, but the condom was a goner.

Sarah was getting frustrated. "Don't you have another one?"

"No," Noah admitted.

"What happened to the Boy Scout Motto?" Sarah teased.

"I was in Adventure Guides," Noah replied before throwing the broken condom aside. But Noah wasn't giving up just yet. He opened the night stand.

"Wait. Here we go," he declared triumphantly. He pulled out a condom and showed it to Sarah.

"Ewwww. No way." Sarah was repulsed by the mere thought of it.

"What?"

"I'm not doing it with Mr. Rosenbaum's condom inside of me!"

"Are you kidding?"

"It's gross." She took it in her hand. "And look," she added. "It's lamb skin. What's lamb skin?"

Noah grabbed the condom back from her and quickly examined it. "It says it's a natural membrane," he offered, trying his best to sell the idea.

"That's the kind that gives you HIV."

"Don't be ridiculous," Noah countered, getting frustrated himself. "It doesn't give you anything, and besides, I don't have anything to give you! You're the only girl I've ever been with!"

But Sarah put her foot down. "I'm sorry. We are *not* using this."

Noah's frustration turned to anger. "Jesus, Sarah. What's the big deal?"

But before she could answer, there was a knock at the door.

"We're in here," Noah called out.

But to Noah's surprise, it was Dylan's voice calling back through the closed door. "Time's up, home slice."

Sarah rolled her eyes. Supremely pissed, Noah got off the bed and stomped over to the door, opening it a crack. Dylan was with the cute girl with the "updoc" on her shirt. Dylan whispered, "The baby's room is empty."

Noah countered, "Then why didn't you just go there, asshole?"

Dylan smiled. "Because my friend..."

The cute girl piped up. "Ashlyn."

Dylan continued, "Ashlyn deserves the best."

Ashlyn smiled, actually flattered by this.

Noah rolled his eyes. But Sarah was already getting dressed and said, "Come on. Let's go." Noah put on his pants but carried his shirt and shoes out of the room with Sarah, as Dylan and Ashlyn entered.

As they passed each other, Noah gave Dylan an evil look reserved only for your cock-blocking best friend. Dylan just smiled.

In the work room, things had gotten really weird really fast. Pike and Ned were now reenacting the light saber duel from *Star Wars,* only they were using a live chainsaw and an electric hedge trimmer. Olaf, Suzanne, and Diaz sat on the couch cheering them on.

Ned spoke with his best Darth Vader voice: "When I left you, I was but the learner; now I am the master."

Pike replied with an English Obi-Wan Kenobi accent: "Only a master of evil, Darth."

Then the two swung their giant power tools at each other. The blades clashed with a tremendous screech of grinding metal. Almost immediately, Pike's chainsaw was deflected onto the couch, *ripping into the cushion* and almost killing Olaf who dove out of the way just in time.

With his weird Norwegian accent, and over the din of the chainsaw still chewing into the couch, Olaf screamed, "What the fuck, Rasshøl?!"

Back in the rec room, Walker and Patience still hadn't moved off the couch through the entire bulk of Playlist #44, which was now blasting that M.I.A. song from *Slumdog Millionaire.* Walker had an endless supply of open-ended questions, from Patience's possible college major ("Maybe English Lit") to whether a private high school education was worth the cost ("Yes"). The conversation was light and superficial, and if this were a talk show, Walker would have made Patience's publicist very happy.

But it wasn't a talk show, and Patience was growing restless. "I'm going to France for the summer," she threw out there. "I'm leaving on Tuesday."

She leaned in once more with a smile, a last ditch effort at getting

Walker to make a move.

But she might as well have been speaking French because Walker merely replied, "Wow, that sounds amazing. I've always wanted to see Paris."

Walker was giving her nothing so Patience simply gave up.

Great, she thought. *I'm stuck with the one gay guy in the whole party.* She leaned back, disappointed.

Without really thinking about it, Sarah and Noah had gone into the baby's room as Dylan had suggested, and now they were lying down on a baby blanket on the floor next to the crib. But the mood was ruined, and they were just leaning on their elbows facing each other. Any hope of reviving the romance was a long-shot, Noah estimated.

"So now what?" Sarah asked.

Noah kissed her. "We can still do *other* things," he said, full of innuendo.

And to Noah's surprise, that's exactly what Sarah wanted to hear. She smiled and started taking off her pants.

Noah was confused. As her jeans were midway down her legs, Noah interrupted. "Uh, no. That's not what I meant."

Sarah immediately got the message. "Oh, so *your* condom breaks so now I have to service you?"

Noah looked at her impishly, like, *Pretty much.*

Sarah was not amused.

The power tools now off, Pike tried fruitlessly to stuff the foam back into the destroyed cushion, but the couch was nearly cut in two. The weed was spent and the others looked around for something else to amuse their addled brains. Suzanne found a small plastic speaker and started fiddling with it. Suddenly, a voice came through the speaker.

It was Sarah. "Why can't you ever go down on me? Did it ever occur to you that I like to get oral sex, too?"

The stoners all stopped in their tracks and looked at each other.

"Oh, my God," Suzanne said, stunned. She giggled uncontrollably and covered her mouth with her hand. Pike grabbed what was clearly a baby monitor from her and turned up the volume.

Noah spoke. "All right, all right. I'll do it."

The five stoners huddled together on the caved-in couch to listen to the drama unfold, like an old-time radio show.

"If it's too disgusting for you," Sarah yelled at Noah, "don't do me any favors. Like having your dick in my mouth is a slice of heaven."

Noah knew there was only one way out of this: south.

"Come here," he said lovingly. He took Sarah into his arms and started kissing her. She held out for a moment to make her point, then finally kissed him back.

Neither of them noticed the red light on the baby monitor sitting on the dresser. Noah kissed Sarah's neck to warm her up, then moved down her torso in the predictable journey to the promised land.

Meanwhile, back on the couch, Patience's body language had completely changed. Any idiot could see she was bored, but Walker plowed on. "So, are you on Facebook?"

Just then, Pike burst into the room holding the baby monitor over his head like a trophy. The other stoners followed close behind, still laughing their asses off. Apparently, they had collectively decided this was simply too good to keep to themselves. Over the monitor, Sarah was moaning, "That's it. Right there, babe. Lick my kitty." And as her moans of ecstasy grew louder, the room went silent and everyone gathered around to listen.

In the baby's room, Noah was doing a pretty solid job getting Sarah off.

"Yes! God, yes! Yes! Lick my kitty!"

The "kitty" thing was nothing new to Noah. Every girl must call her vagina *something*, he thought the first time he heard Sarah say it. By now, it didn't even occur to him that it sounded kind of funny. But to the forty-odd people in the rec room downstairs, listening to the proverbial blow by blow, it was downright hilarious.

"Lick my kitty! Lick my kitty!" Sarah screamed as she got closer and closer.

The whole rec room was now chanting: "Lick her kitty! Lick her kitty!"

Pike, who obviously had been heavily into *Star Wars* before taking up pot, quoted that guy in the attack squadron in the final battle against the Death Star: "Stay on target."

More moans, louder, faster.

Suzanne gave her expert opinion, "She's almost there..."

"Stay on target," Pike repeated.

"Lick my kitty!"

"Almost…"

"Stay on target…"

Sarah screamed, "Yes! Yes! *Yes!!!*"

A moment of silence, then the rec room erupted with applause.

Marco, ever the one to recognize a money-making opportunity, checked his stopwatch. "Okay, who had five oh two?" A football player raised his hand and Marco paid him the impromptu pool money.

Sarah and Noah got dressed and left the baby's room. Sarah was in a good mood now and Noah felt genuinely happy to have brought so much pleasure to her. As they walked along the upstairs hallway, some people chuckled at them. One random dude with a goatee made claws at Sarah and meowed.

Sarah looked at Noah a little confused, but also a tiny bit nervous. The two headed downstairs to the first floor where they passed other people who also meowed at her. Sarah's fears were swelling. "What's going on here?"

"I have no idea," Noah replied.

They headed down the next staircase to the basement. As they made it halfway, the room erupted in applause. Sarah and Noah still had no idea what was going on, until Marco shouted, "Lick my kitty! Lick my kitty!" He showed them the baby monitor and Sarah turned crimson.

"Oh, my God," she eked out.

Sarah turned around and ran back upstairs. Noah raced after her.

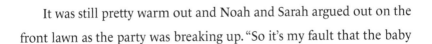

It was still pretty warm out and Noah and Sarah argued out on the front lawn as the party was breaking up. "So it's my fault that the baby monitor was on?" Noah asked defensively. "How was I supposed to know?"

"If you had a stupid back-up condom none of this would have happened!"

Noah was sick of her stupid logic. "Who cares anyway? In ten days you're never going to see any of these people again!"

Sarah stared right into his eyes. "You mean like you?"

Oops.

Noah felt like he'd been outmaneuvered and quickly backtracked. "No, that's not what I meant." He looked down at the ground, barely able to get out, "But we should be realistic."

Sarah started to tear up.

Noah explained, "You're going to Madison. I'll be halfway across the country."

"They don't have Spring Break at Brown?" Sarah asked accusingly.

"They do, it's just..." Noah didn't know if he should go there, but if they couldn't be honest with each other, then what's the point? "We fight all the time..."

A tear streamed down her cheek. "If you want to break up with me, just say so."

But Noah didn't say anything, which was actually worse. She had her answer. The silence was interrupted by a car honking for Sarah.

"Fine. Whatever." She turned to leave.

Noah felt like an asshole. "Wait. Sarah—"

But it was too late. Sarah ran over to her friend's waiting car and got in.

Noah watched them drive off, then trudged over to the driveway where Pike and Dylan were waiting for Walker to say goodbye to Patience.

"It was really great talking to you tonight," Walker said, content in his mind that he had flawlessly executed step one of a ninety-three-part plan.

"Yeah, me, too," Patience responded politely.

Walker added, "Have fun in France," proving to her what a good listener he was.

"Thanks." She shifted uncomfortably.

"So... I'll email you," Walker confirmed. He leaned in to hug her at the same time she extended a hand to shake in a classic-sitcom awkward moment. Walker quickly adjusted and shook her hand.

And then she was gone.

Walker joined the other three guys.

"Pathetic," Dylan launched into him. "Fucking pathetic."

Walker still didn't get it. "What?"

Noah was in no mood to watch Dylan pick on Walker. "Give him a break."

Dylan looked at Noah like, *What's your problem?*

Pike changed the subject. "Anyone hungry? I'm starving."

CHAPTER SIX

THE STEAK AND Egg Kitchen was a throw-back to a simpler time, when grease was one of the four major food groups, and if you got sick from eating a $4.99 T-bone then that was your problem, not theirs. The simple brick building in the West Hartford Center housed some of the surliest waitresses and crunchiest pancakes in town. But the Steak and Egg Kitchen was also the only place in town that was open twenty-four hours.

Dylan and Pike were busy chewing out Walker while Noah moped over his scrambled eggs. "The girl goes to Choate, so you know she's gotta be all coked up," Dylan theorized.

"True dat," Pike affirmed.

Walker shook his head. "I don't think she was—"

But Dylan didn't let him finish. "And she's going to France, *home* of the dirty whore. Leaving on Tuesday, mind you, so whatever happens is totally guilt-free."

Walker was starting to see the picture they were painting of sweet

Patience.

"Don't forget Wellesley," Pike added with a mouthful of cube steak, "so chances are she's into chicks as well."

Walker's mind raced with the possibilities that entailed.

Dylan took Walker by the shoulder. "She didn't know anybody at the party." Walker thought back on the evening. Dylan continued, "Admit it, this girl was giving you the green light to use and abuse her like the cheap slut that she is."

Without looking up, Pike gave an amen, "He ain't lyin'." He started demolishing the stack of pancakes on the side plate next to his cube steak.

Walker went over it in his mind and after weighing all the possibilities, he suddenly realized that they were absolutely right. He sunk into his seat. "Fuck."

Dylan laughed. "Did you at least get her info?"

"I got her email," Walker remembered hopefully, brightening his mood like maybe all wasn't lost. "I told her when she gets back I would make her a lasagna."

Pike and Dylan looked at each other for a moment, then burst out laughing.

Walker didn't get the joke. "What?" he asked.

But Dylan just rubbed his hair, like you would do to a little kid who just said something cute. "Eat your pancakes."

Walker was now officially depressed.

"And you," Dylan turned to Noah. "Will you stop crying? You did what you had to do."

"I don't know," Noah tried to convince himself. "We didn't officially break up or anything."

Not known for his tact, Pike blurted out, "I bet she delists you on Facebook."

Noah knew he was right. It was over.

Dylan tried to cheer him up. "You're eighteen. What were you going to do, get married? This isn't West Virginia."

"I know. But still." Noah looked up. "We love each other."

"And you've been fighting for months," Dylan reminded him. "I'm just looking out for you, man. Once you've been with other girls—"

Noah leapt on that statement. "What does that matter? Sarah and I have had sex almost ninety times." No one thought it was weird that Noah had apparently been counting.

"Variety," Pike explained, his mouth full of pancakes.

"Exactly," Dylan seconded. "Other girls will give you perspective."

Walker piped up, taking Noah's side in this debate. "Don't listen to them. I'd love to be with a girl like Sarah."

"You'd love to be with a girl who's alive," Dylan shot back.

"And has two legs," Pike added.

Dylan considered. "I don't think that matters to Walker." He turned to him thoughtfully. "You wouldn't nail a hot chick with one leg?"

Walker gave them both a *ha ha* fake smile, but Dylan wasn't done giving him shit. "I mean, *after* you make her a lasagna, of course."

"Shut up," Walker said. He threw a tub of grape jelly at Dylan and the four of them broke out laughing.

It was small moments like this—the four best friends eating gristle at two a.m., playfully ribbing each other, and sharing a laugh—that they'd remember forever. And for Dylan, he couldn't imagine being anywhere else.

Before crashing for the night, Noah checked Sarah's Facebook profile. Under "News Feed" it said, "Sarah is now single," complete with the broken heart icon. Dejected, Noah clicked off his iPhone and just sat there, staring into the darkness.

Walker was on Facebook as well, but Walker was masturbating to the profile picture of Patience, the girl from the party.

When Pike got home and did *his* bedtime e-ritual, he opened a message from Marco with the subject, "Couch," and his eyes went wide.

After dropping off the guys, Dylan pulled the Cube into his driveway and parked next to a pick-up truck emblazoned with "Glasco Paving." Inside, Dylan found his dad asleep on the couch with ESPN on. Dylan turned off the TV and covered his dad with a blanket before heading into his bedroom.

Dylan didn't hate his dad. He had just learned to live without him. But that didn't mean his dad knew how to live without Dylan. The poor bastard didn't know how to cook. Hell, he barely knew how to use the DVR. Dylan wondered what his dad was going to do when Dylan left.

Dylan brushed his teeth and changed for bed. But for some reason he wasn't tired. He was deep in thought. Then, an idea struck him. He pulled out his phone and started a text message.

CHAPTER SEVEN

By FIFTH PERIOD Monday, Dylan was in the cafeteria with his friends, still busy texting. The others didn't seem to care what Dylan was up to—they were focused on their pepperoni pizzas and discussing plans for Beach Weekend.

"So I emailed Patience," Walker began. "She didn't write back."

Noah broke the news, "Dude, that ship has sailed."

"Why don't you just fuck Natalie?" Pike suggested, just trying to be helpful.

"Natalie's my cousin," Walker replied, with the *asshole* left implied.

Pike was undeterred. "Or that weird girl." Sure enough, a weird-looking girl sat alone eating edamame. She had a nice body, and a cute face under her heavy makeup and eyeliner, but she always sat by herself and dressed in flannel as if Nirvana were still awesome.

Still, even for Walker it was a pass. "Yeah, I'll get right on that."

Dylan was still furiously texting when Walker moved on to a moment of self-reflection. "I think I just need to accept that high school is over and I'll make a fresh start next year in college."

"Sounds like a plan," Noah humored him.

Pike was still brainstorming. "Hey, Suzanne will sleep with you if you buy her some weed."

Walker perked up, considering. "Is she going to Marco's for Beach Weekend?"

But before Pike could figure out how to make that happen, Dylan finally finished on the phone and held it up triumphantly. "Cancel your Brazilian waxes, gentlemen. Welcome to Beach Weekend 2.0."

That got their attention. Even if they had no idea what he was talking about, it sounded promising.

Dylan continued, "We're not going to Marco's. We're going into the city."

"Hartford?" Walker inquired.

"New York, dumbass." Dylan started going over the texts. "My friend Pete just told me about a massive party in the city Friday night."

Pike racked his brain. "Is he that guy from the ski trip? The one with three balls?"

"Yeah," Dylan replied.

Noah looked concerned. "But what about Marco's?"

"Fuck Marco's," Dylan countered. "This is Stark Raving Mad 2012. It's in an abandoned warehouse. There's going to be close to a thousand people there."

Pike's eyes lit up. "Perfect. I can pick up some weed in the city."

"You don't have enough weed?" Walker wondered aloud.

"Marco says I owe him twelve hundred bucks for that piece of shit couch."

"That's fucking bullshit," Walker said, trying to sound supportive.

"I know," Pike lamented. "But he said I could pay him back in weed."

Noah was still stuck on the basic premise. "Guys, we can't miss the last big party of high school."

"High school is over, my man," Dylan proclaimed, then added, "Ask your doctor what not being a pussy can do for you." Dylan was very pleased with himself for coming up with that last part.

But Noah wasn't sure.

Dylan tried to ice the cake. "We're talking about New York City. No ID required. Topless bars. Bottomless drinks. And the loosest sluts on the Strip." Dylan was on fire with catchy sayings.

But he could see that Noah was still down in the dumps and that he had to cheer him up before he would agree to anything. "Look, I get it." He looked at Noah sympathetically. "But it's over between you and Sarah. You need to move on. And we are going to help you do just that."

The way Dylan figured, there was something in it for everyone. They'd get Pike some pot, get Walker laid, and get Noah to forget about Sarah. "It'll be our last big hurrah of high school."

Noah was stubborn. "What's the hurry? We have the whole summer to party."

Dylan flinched so slightly that the guys didn't even notice. They *didn't* have the whole summer, even if Dylan wasn't ready yet to tell his friends why.

Noah still wasn't convinced. Sure, a weekend in New York with the guys would probably be pretty awesome. But Noah wanted to be with Sarah and Sarah was going to be at Marco's. He didn't care that they had broken up. He wanted to spend the last weekend of high school with the guys *and* her.

Before they could discuss it any further, Marco's bouncer friend

Chuck walked by with his football brethren. He led with his standard greeting, "S'up, ladies," then for absolutely no reason whatsoever proceeded to give Walker a titty-twister.

Walker screamed. "Ow! That hurt, asshole!"

Noah stepped up to defend Walker. "Stop being a dick, Chuck."

Chuck came back with an ever-so-witty retort, "I'm sorry, ahomosayswhat?"

Noah just rolled his eyes. It was the oldest one in the book and Noah wasn't going to let Chuck have the satisfaction. "Excuse me? Didn't quite catch that."

Chuck repeated, "Ahomosayswhat?" a few times, hoping to trick Noah, but Noah was about a hundred IQ points smarter than Chuck and just replied, "Hmm. Nope. Not understanding. You know, you really need to enunciate."

Frustrated, Chuck finally just tipped over Noah's can of Sierra Mist, laughed, and yelled, "Homo!"

Noah righted his can and threw a napkin onto the spill. "Well played," he said sarcastically.

Chuck received a high-five from his buddies for a job well done and headed out.

Noah turned to Dylan and without any further debate, said merely, "All right. I'm in."

Dylan smiled.

CHAPTER EIGHT

THE NEXT FOUR days went by slowly. It was finals after all, and even though they were all into great colleges, they still had to pass. Add to that the usual end-of-year assemblies, extra-curricular activity wrap-ups, and locker cleaning, and it made for a long week. But Friday was Senior Skip Day and only the biggest tools in school showed up when the administration practically endorsed this one day of truancy. Most of the seniors would be heading down to Misquamicut for a rowdy party to end all parties at Marco's parents' house. The place was actually pretty sweet—a multi-million-dollar Cape Cod-style beach house with ninety feet of ocean-front sand. But Dylan and the guys had other plans.

Dylan had already picked up Pike and Walker by eleven a.m. and they took their long-ago-assigned seats in the back of the Cube. Dylan pulled into Noah's driveway and honked. Noah came out in no time and in addition to a duffel bag with a change of clothes, he was carrying his book bag.

"What's in the bag?" Walker asked as Noah opened the passenger door.

"Snacks." Noah pulled out a bag of Fritos and tossed it to Pike.

"Su-weet!" Pike chirped, and Noah smiled.

"And Dylan's yearbook," Noah added.

Dylan chided him, "Dude, you're not going to have time to sit around signing my yearbook."

"Well, just in case," Noah replied as he closed the door.

Now that Noah was in place riding shotgun, the car felt whole. Dylan looked at his three friends and knew this weekend was going to be special. They all knew they were about to have fun, maybe even have the adventure of a lifetime. But Dylan alone had the prescience to appreciate that he was *making* a moment *right now*. And that for the rest of his life he would only be able to look back on this moment as a fond memory. He alone knew this was the end of an era, the last time the guys would be together in this way.

"Songs will be sung of our exploits here today," Pike boomed.

Noah put on his sunglasses. "All right. Let's do this."

"There you go," Dylan encouraged. "Now once more with feeling."

"New York City!" Noah screamed, with feeling.

"New York City!!!" Walker echoed.

"NEW YORK CITY!!!" the four of them screamed at the top of their lungs.

Dylan pulled out onto the street and the memory officially began.

As they cruised south down I-91 to Green Day's "21 Guns," Pike was smoking weed in the back seat, Walker had his window rolled down to avoid the smoke, Noah was reading through Dylan's yearbook, and

Dylan was pontificating.

"I'm just saying," Dylan began, "the whole boyfriend-girlfriend thing is just so old-fashioned. As long as there's a steady stream of beautiful girls willing to engage in no-strings sex, what's the point of pinning Sally Merriweather with your pledge pin?"

"Who the fuck is Sally Merriweather?" Pike interjected from the back seat. Everyone ignored him.

"Not everyone is made like you, Dylan," Noah countered. "Some guys actually like getting to know a girl. Having a relationship."

"Licking the kitty," Dylan jabbed.

The guys laughed and even Noah couldn't help but smile. Then Noah saw something noteworthy in Dylan's yearbook. "Check this out. Libby Hoechner wrote, 'Keep in touch.' That's it, just 'keep in touch.'" Noah acted as if he was personally offended by her lack of imagination.

Walker joined in, "I'm sure you and Libby will be BFFs for years to come."

But Dylan jumped to Libby's defense, "Hey, Libby Hoechner gave me my first blow job," as if that justified the no-frills message.

Then Dylan looked back at Walker for a second. "You remember your first blow job, Walker?"

Walker thought back. Of course he remembered. It was his first and only blow job and when he called the promiscuous, pill-popping Amy Waverly the next day, she had no memory of the event. Still, it was the best ten seconds of Walker's life.

"Uh huh, I guess so," Walker answered with trepidation.

"How'd it taste?" was the punch line Dylan delivered with impeccable comic timing. He laughed his ass off and Noah and Pike joined in.

Walker was used to being teased and took the ribbing good-naturedly.

Noah flipped to another page. "Look at this one from Karla Feeny. 'Congrads' with a 'd,' 'I am going to miss you so much next year.' Really? I mean, have you ever even said two words to Karla Feeny since junior high?"

"It's just something you say," Dylan chastised. "Stop being so critical."

"Here's another one. Amy Ryan wrote, 'Remember that time at Marco's house? You were so drunk.'" Noah laughed, "Yeah, can you be a little more specific?"

Noah opened the door with all this yearbook talk and Dylan took the opportunity to turn it back on him. "Okay, Smart Guy, so what are you going to write in my yearbook?"

"I don't know. But we're best friends. I want to write something special."

"Wow, that was really gay," Dylan teased. "Seriously, you don't want to wait until college to come out of the closet?"

"Shut up," Noah shot back with a smile.

"Come here," Dylan apologized and facetiously leaned in to kiss him. Noah pushed him away. The car swerved slightly and Dylan returned to the wheel with a laugh.

Then Pike saw something. "Check it out. Eight o'clock." It was a car full of hot girls in bikinis passing them on their left in a VW Bug convertible.

Like a cheetah spotting a car full of gazelles, Dylan immediately sped up to match their highway speed. He rolled down his window and yelled to be heard over the wind, "Where you girls headed?"

A cute girl with long blonde hair and a pink bikini yelled back from the passenger seat, "Old Lyme!"

Dylan kept one eye on the road and the other eye on this girl's ample cleavage. He pouted, "No, come with us! We're heading into the city!"

"Sorry!" she laughed.

Dylan loved flirting, but in times like this you really just have to get to the point. "At least show us your tits!"

Walker gasped. "Dylan!"

"Shh! Shh!" Dylan cautioned. "I think they're going to do it."

And sure enough, the girl appeared to be discussing the idea with her friends.

Dylan sensed they were on the fence so he pushed them in the right direction with, "Come on! You know you want to!" Then he flashed them his million-dollar smile.

Then... the four girls lifted their bikini tops and flashed their tits.

The guys couldn't believe it. They were in awe, giggling like little boys. And the girls were laughing, too, because, as savvy men know, good girls love being bad.

Then, as if this weren't a big enough victory, Dylan shouted across the asphalt, "Can my friend put his face in your tits?"

The girl looked at him like he was crazy, but crazy was just what she was in the mood for.

Dylan inched his car closer to the Bug without hitting it.

And even Walker, sitting behind Dylan, didn't need any further prodding on this one. He rolled his window down and stuck his head out.

The cars were close enough now that the blonde girl no longer in a pink bikini grabbed Walker's head and kissed him. Then she forced his head down into her tits and Walker got a mouth full. All this at sixty-five miles an hour.

Suddenly, *honk!*

Dylan swerved right and Walker fell back into the Cube. They looked behind them to see... *a school bus*, filled with horny middle-school boys with their noses pressed up against the windows.

The guys laughed their asses off. The girls quickly pulled their tops back on and sped off.

Dylan called after them, "Aw, come on! Where are you going?" But the fun was over, so Dylan honked his horn in appreciation as the girls disappeared down the highway.

Dylan saw Walker's face in the rear view mirror. He was smiling ear to ear. "That was awesome," he beamed.

And Dylan, ever the good friend, made sure this was a teaching moment: "You see? A little initiative goes a long way."

The guys approached New Haven and took the exit onto 95 South. By now they were eating McDonald's, listening to Pike's eclectic iMix (currently playing: Daft Punk's "Digital Love"), and shooting the shit.

Soon-to-be Ivy Leaguer Noah asked Dylan, "Did you get your fresh-man orientation guide from UConn yet?"

Dylan uncharacteristically avoided eye contact and just muttered, "Uh, no, not yet." Clearly he wasn't ready to talk about his college plans just yet.

Pike bit into his Big Mac. "University of the Pacific, my friends. Miles of sand, hot girls in bikinis as far as the eye can see."

Walker was skeptical. "Yeah, I'm sure they have a great record getting people into law school."

"Maybe not," Pike conceded, "but they have a great record getting guys into pussy." He reached forward and high-fived Dylan who, without looking, had instinctively turned his hand to meet Pike's.

Pike grew philosophical. "We've all been stuck here in West Hartford our whole lives," his tirade began. "But instead of making a break big time, you 'tards are staying right here."

The guys rolled their eyes as Pike continued, "Providence? Boston? UConn? Live the dream, baby. Live the dream." Supremely proud of himself, he took a sip of his milkshake.

The other three gave him a collective *whatever* look.

―――――――――――――

In just under an hour they crossed the border into New York State, and the guys sat in silence for a while owing primarily to the fact that the universally awesome "Such Great Heights" by the Postal Service came on in the shuffle.

Despite Dylan's spotty driving record, the Cube felt safe as it raced down the highway. Noah and Dylan had been friends the longest, since kindergarten; but even Pike, who had joined the gang the most recently (in ninth grade), felt like the four of them were a family. And the family felt safe.

They were excited to go off to college, of course. All guys build up college as a utopian existence with insane parties, unlimited drinking, sexually adventuresome girls, and most importantly, unbridled freedom. The freedom to blow off classes if you're hung over. The freedom to sleep until noon, if that's what your body's schedule dictates. And the freedom to pursue interests both profound and mundane. No one is going to stop you from joining the unicycle club or tell you you can't take Philosophy 355, "The Perception of Color," if that's what floats your boat. Maybe deep down they knew college wasn't really going to be like *Animal House*, but they were still excited to get out of West Hartford and move on to the next chapter in their lives.

Yet part of graduating high school was also pretty scary. It was the part they didn't show you in *American Pie* movies and on *Greek*. Maybe it didn't occur to them in this moment as the electronic chorus blared, "Everything looks perfect from far away," but the guys hadn't had to make new friends since they were in elementary school. Leaving home was going to be the biggest, most traumatic event of their lives. But right now, in the Cube, with each other, they felt invincible.

The song ended, and soon the Cube was cruising down the Saw Mill Parkway. When they finally saw a sign that read "Manhattan," the guys cheered.

CHAPTER NINE

THE GUYS ARRIVED in Manhattan just after lunch and parked in a garage near Times Square. Sure, it was a little clichéd and touristy but the guys *were* tourists. Plus, even at their age, it was still pretty fucking cool to take in the sights, sounds, and smells of the city.

As they walked down Broadway, Walker was eyeing some really reasonably-priced Rolexes when Dylan literally stopped and turned as four tall, European-looking models walked by. Dylan nudged Noah and soon the guys were admiring the view of these incredible babes walking by. Deep down, the other three felt comforted that there were still women in the world who were out of even the mighty Dylan's league.

As they turned up 40th Street, Pike noticed a crowd gathered around a folding table and suggested they check it out. It was a handsome young African-American gentleman dealing three-card monte.

"Keep your eye on the lady," he preached, showing the crowd the queen of hearts amid two black aces. Then he started tossing the cards back and forth, slowly enough so that any idiot could keep track of the queen. He practically sang, "Round and round, there she goes, where she lands, nobody knows." He stopped the deal and looked up at the black guy in front of him with a fist full of money.

Pike whispered to Noah, "In the middle."

The dealer overheard Pike and said, "Good eye, good eye. But is he right?"

The man with the cash glanced back at Pike and must have been impressed with his powers of observation because he said, "I think he's right. Twenty bucks in the middle."

He laid down a twenty and the dealer flipped over the middle card. It was the queen.

"Damn, you're good," the dealer complimented Pike. He paid out twenty dollars to his celebrating shill and added convincingly, "You're gonna bankrupt me, man."

The dealer started up the routine again, showing the queen and two aces to the crowd like before. "Round and round, there she goes, where she lands, nobody knows."

The queen was obviously on the left this time but the shill apparently still needed Pike's help because he turned to him and asked, "Which one, man?"

"On the left," Pike whispered confidently.

"You heard him," the shill gloated. "Twenty on the left."

Sure enough, that was the queen. The dealer pretended to curse his bad luck and paid the shill, now pretending to be ecstatic. The shill flashed his wad of cash in the other guy's face. "Pleasure doin' business with you," the shill bragged. "Now I've got some business to attend to with a t-bone at Sizzler."

He laughed and headed down 40th Street.

Pike had that look in his eye. The guys had seen it far too many times, like right before he jumped off Sarah's roof onto a trampoline floating in her swimming pool. It was a surprisingly intense stare, given that Pike was still high. And it meant that he was about to do something stupid.

"Who's next? Who's next?" the dealer called out like a carnival barker. "Step right up." Then he turned to Pike. "How about it, Eagle Eyes? You want to take a shot?"

"I'll play," Pike said as he reached for his wallet.

Noah grabbed his arm, and whispered, "Dude, are you serious? It's a scam."

"That guy just won," Pike reasoned. "I can beat him."

"Don't be stupid," Walker seconded.

"Pike—" Dylan thirded.

But Pike could not be talked down, so Noah shook his head and let him go.

"Let's do this."

The dealer smiled and began his routine, showing the queen, throwing the cards around slowly enough that you could easily follow it, and singing his little "round and round" song. He stopped and Pike smiled. The queen was obviously in the middle.

"What'cha say, my man?" the dealer said charismatically.

Pike laid down a twenty and stated confidently, "It's in the middle."

The dealer flipped over an ace and scooped up Pike's money quick as lightning.

Pike couldn't believe it. The queen was there! "But I saw it—"

"Sorry, my friend, you losing your concentration on me now? The queen is a royal bitch and you gots to pay attention."

The other three guys rolled their eyes.

Noah tried one more time to reason with him, speaking slowly, "It's. A. Con."

But Pike was committed to this cause. "No, I can do this."

"Come on, dude," Dylan interrupted, "just give him your wallet and stop wasting our time."

Pike just turned to the dealer. "Let's go again."

"That's the spirit! Do or die, never give up, that's what made this country great." The clichés poured out like a fine bottle of Night Train.

He showed the queen again then began his patter. "Round and round, there she goes, where she winds up, nobody knows."

As the cards jumped back and forth, Walker looked at Noah, like, *Shouldn't we do something?*, but Noah was at a loss for how to convince Pike to abandon this avenue of idiocy.

Dylan summed it up, quietly commenting, "There's no stopping him now."

The cards came to a rest and this time Pike was *sure* the queen was on the left. He threw down another twenty and declared his choice.

The dealer flipped up the card. Ace.

He grabbed Pike's money and Pike turned red. "Fuck! How is he doing that?!"

"You getting sleepy, my man?" the dealer asked, hoping to score a third bet. "I thought we was friends."

Pike reached for his wallet.

Dylan nodded to Noah and together the two of them literally grabbed Pike by both arms.

"Come on, genius," Noah prodded.

The dealer was upset. "Hey, man, what'choo doin'? Ain't this a free country? Ain't a man got a right to make a fair wager?"

But as the guys pulled the livid Pike away, the dealer knew it was over. In a flash, the table was folded up and he and his shills and lookouts were down the street scouting for their next mark.

"No, wait!" Pike pleaded, "I know how he's doing it! Let's go back! Let's go back!"

As he struggled, Dylan pulled him in to a head lock and gave him a friendly noogie, laughing, "You dumb motherfucker."

The guys spent the rest of the afternoon walking through Central Park, checking out the 9/11 Memorial, and exploring Rockefeller Center. At FAO Schwartz, they played laser tag, knocking over displays and causing a scene in the store. As for food, they ate hot dogs and pretzels from a vendor on 38th Street. But by five p.m., it was down to business, and the guys found themselves smoking cigars, drinking beers, and watching the show on the main stage of the Baby Dolls Gentlemen's Club.

It's funny how guys are around strippers. One regiment of strippers could probably end war as we know it because beautiful naked women have a pacifying effect on everyone around. Men of all ages just sit there, mouths slightly ajar, gaping at the sea of breasts and asses. They look hypnotized—how else could the strippers get them to empty their wallets for a no-touch lap dance?

Our guys were no exception. Even Dylan gazed in amazement at the quality and quantity. Occasionally, a particularly stunning one would walk by and one of the guys would point her out to the others. They bought each other lap dances, as was the custom, as if buying a lap dance for a friend were less seedy than buying one for yourself. Some nonverbal clues were needed so the interested party could convey his preference to the buyer, but at a place like Baby Dolls there weren't too many bad choices.

Walker scored the most dances. It was fun to watch him squirm and turn red when a girl shook her ass in his face or squeezed her breasts together to grab a dollar bill from his teeth. After a few minutes, Def Leppard's "Pour Some Sugar on Me" ended (the guys wondered if strip club DJs *ever* updated their playlists) and Walker needed a break.

Dylan was just about to call the waitress over for another round when Pike's eyes went wide. Coming into the club was Chuck Zambrelli with his football buddies.

"No way," Pike gasped, in utter disbelief.

But it *was* Chuck and he was headed right toward them. After a proverbial double-take, Chuck exclaimed, "Holy shit! It's the itty bitty limp dick committee."

After some congratulatory high-fives from his buddies, Chuck followed it up with his trademark, "S'up, ladies?"

Dylan was a little buzzed and decided it was finally time to address the issue that had irked the entire school for years. "Look, Chuck. We're about to graduate. You think you could retire the 's'up, ladies?' line?"

"Whatever, dude."

"No, seriously," Dylan continued. "I think you should segue to 'wassuuuuup!'" he said with an "urban" flair, calling back that decade-old catch-phrase from those Budweiser commercials that took the country by storm.

But Chuck seemed unfamiliar with the concept, so Dylan put the exclamation on the point: "That'll go over like gangbusters at Manchester Community College next year."

Zing.

Chuck was actually kind of offended. You could tell by the tone of his "Fuck you."

Chuck retreated back to his buddies who were already ordering beers from a not-quite-hot-enough waitress.

Noah turned to Dylan and failed to whisper, "You're giving him too much credit. You still have to know how to read to get in to Manchester."

The guys all shared a laugh, until Chuck turned back to face them.

Oops.

They stopped laughing.

But Chuck didn't look mad. He looked hurt.

"Hey, I heard that. And for your information, I'm dyslexic, man."

The guys looked at each other. That was not expected.

Chuck continued, starting to get a little emotional, "So excuse me if I'm not going to a fucking Ivy League school, asshole, but reading is really hard work for me and it doesn't mean I'm stupid."

Chuck just stood there looking embarrassed, and this only made the guys feel even more like shit.

"I'm sorry, man," Noah apologized.

"Yeah, we didn't know," Dylan said, looking contrite as well.

"Have you tried 'Hooked on Phonics'?" Walker added, sincerely trying to be helpful.

Dylan elbowed him.

Chuck took a deep, pained breath.

Dylan knew one way to bury the hatchet for good. "Look, man. Let us buy you a lap dance. No hard feelings?"

Chuck tried to get past his surge of emotions. "Yeah, okay."

Dylan patted him on the back and said, "There you go. Class of 2012 has to stick together, right?"

Chuck nodded, still too choked up to speak. Dylan escorted him through the club to go find a stripper.

"Awk-ward," Walker chirped under his breath.

Five minutes and one airplay of Foreigner's "Hot Blooded" later, Chuck explained over a Long Island Ice Tea that he and Marco had had a falling out. It seemed that Chuck had worked as Marco's personal bouncer all these years for no pay, just free entry into the parties. But after four years Chuck finally realized that he never got to *go* to any of the parties because he was always standing at the front door all night long. So Chuck asked Marco if he could just attend Beach Weekend without working the door. He even offered to bring the customary alcohol.

But Marco flew into a rage. "You ungrateful bastard!" he shouted, like he'd rescued Chuck from an animal shelter and now Chuck was refusing to guard the junkyard. "Who's gonna man the door?"

"Dunno," Chuck replied, then had the nerve to ask, "Why does there need to be a bouncer at the door anyway? I mean, who's gonna drive all the way down to Rhode Island just to crash your party?"

Marco just glared at him. "Look, I'll make it simple for you," Marco threatened, "Either you work the door or you don't show up."

"What a dick," Dylan said sympathetically.

So, long story long, Chuck discussed it with the rest of the team and they took a vote to support Chuck and boycott Marco's. Steve Wasnicki's brother lived in the city and the rest was history.

The guys sat and listened, and it occurred to Noah that this was the longest conversation he'd ever had with Chuck Zambrelli. He mentioned that fact to Pike in the men's room during a piss break. The end of high school really did mend fences and break down barriers.

"Strange days indeed," Pike agreed.

CHAPTER TEN

AFTER A FEW more lap dances and the free dinner buffet at Baby Dolls, the guys said farewell to Chuck and the rest of the football team and headed out to their next destination of the evening. It was a bit far, so the guys picked up the car from the garage, paid the shocking forty-six dollar fee, and headed west.

The Manhattan neighborhoods changed quickly, and soon they arrived at a sketchy neighborhood near the Lincoln Tunnel. Pike checked the address on his phone.

"There," he pointed.

Dylan rolled up in front of an apartment building that sat on top of A-1 Bail Bonds. *Plenty of parking in this neighborhood*, he thought.

Walker looked out through the window. Some unsavory characters were milling around in front of a boarded-up building.

"You sure this is a good idea?" he asked.

"It's fine," Pike assured him. "Ned knows this guy personally."

"Where does he know him from?" Dylan wondered aloud. "Juvie?"

Pike became defensive. "This is high grade Jamaican Sinsemilla. You can't get this shit in Connecticut."

"You can't get ebola there either," Noah shot back.

But Pike needed this weed to pay Marco back for the couch he had sawed in half, so the discussion was moot. Pike considered blowing Marco off—after all, what could he do if Pike didn't pay?—but then Pike came up with a list of about twenty pretty awful things Marco could and would do, not the least of which was to post the literally hundreds of photos of Pike smoking a bong that Marco had taken over the years. Marco was a vindictive motherfucker, and it was simply better to pay him for the couch than lose sleep wondering when the knife was going to slit your throat.

Besides, the twelve hundred dollars of pot only cost nine hundred in the city.

"Come on," Pike ordered as he opened his door.

The guys rolled their eyes and got out as well.

Dylan locked the car, then checked the handle manually to make sure. As they made their way toward the apartment building, Walker surreptitiously moved his wallet from his back pocket to his front. They reached the front steps and Pike examined the names on the buzzer.

"Here we go," he said to himself and pushed 3F.

"Hola" came a man's voice from the speaker.

"Hey. It's Pike. Ned's friend."

"Como?"

"Ned Carney? From Connecticut?"

Pike wondered if maybe Ned forgot to text the guy. That certainly wouldn't be surprising.

But then, without further discussion, the buzzer sounded.

Pike looked at the other guys, shrugged, and opened the door.

They walked up to the third floor—there was no elevator—and Pike knocked on 3F. After a moment, the door opened to reveal Jesus, a fairly scrawny Hispanic kid not much older than they were.

Jesus was a small time drug dealer, and in his barely-furnished apartment were a couple of guys playing Wii Bowling, a cute girl watching the video game, a case of fire extinguishers, and a guy passed out in the corner. (One of the video game guys was short and fat, the other tall and skinny, like an Hispanic Laurel and Hardy.) Jesus motioned for them to enter and Pike cautiously led the guys in. They tried not to look nervous, but they had seen too many movies where guys in this situation got shot, or worse, not to be a little on edge.

Jesus just stood there until Pike started the conversation. "What up, man. Ned said you might have something for me...?"

Jesus looked him over. "You got the money?"

Pike pulled out a wad of cash from his jeans and handed it over. "Here you go."

As Jesus counted it, Walker motioned toward the guy passed out in the corner and whispered to Noah, "I think that guy's dead."

Walker could have been right, but Noah didn't think it prudent to make too much conversation here, so he motioned for Walker to zip it. Dylan squinted to get a better look.

Satisfied with the count, Jesus whistled to one of the guys playing the video game (the skinny one) and he whipped a brick of marijuana over to Jesus. "Here you go, amigo," Jesus said as he handed it over to Pike. "Pleasure doing business with you."

With the business transaction concluded, Jesus's whole demeanor changed. Suddenly, he smiled and patted Pike on the back.

Pike picked up on it. "Should we celebrate this new relationship?"

Now Jesus really was his new best friend. "Fuck yeah, man. Fire it up."

While all this was going on, Dylan stealthily sidled over to the passed out guy and lightly kicked him. He didn't move.

***

Twenty minutes later, Pike, Jesus, the cute girl, and Señores Laurel and Hardy sat on the couch passing a fat joint. Dylan, Noah, and Walker stood nearby drinking beers.

"This is good shit," Pike commented after a particularly big hit.

Jesus laughed, "You are fucked up, man."

Pike laughed as well and pulled out his phone. He took a picture of the pot and emailed it to Ned. "Ned is going to fucking love this," Pike said of the picture, not the pot, which unfortunately was earmarked for Marco.

Across the room, Walker was trying to steal a glance at the cute girl. Unfortunately, she looked up right then and their eyes met. Walker quickly looked away but it was too late; she had caught him obviously checking her out. She smiled playfully.

"She's cute," Noah commented.

"Should I go talk to her? What do I say?" Walker always made everything so complicated.

Dylan was the voice of reason, reassuring Walker, "She's stoned. You don't need to say anything. Just stick your tongue down her throat."

"Out of the blue?" Walker panicked, "What if she—"

Frustrated, Dylan just *slapped Walker across the face.*

"Owww! That fucking hurt!"

"Proof that non-verbal communication works." And with that, Dylan pushed Walker away, toward the couch.

Walker stumbled over to the girl who looked up expectantly. "Can I sit here?" he asked nervously.

She just nodded and Pike moved over to let Walker sit between him and the girl.

Walker looked over at Dylan for moral support. Dylan gave him a *trust me* look.

Jesus passed her the joint. She took a big hit and passed it to Walker. But instead of partaking, he just passed it on to Pike, turned to her, and *kissed her*!

He came up for air and looked at her nervously, like, *Is she going to kick me in the balls?* But all she did was exhale a huge breath of pot smoke.

Walker realized his error and apologized, "Sorry, I—"

But she just laughed and kissed Walker back.

Sure, she was surprised, but as predicted, she was totally fine with it. They started making out.

"I can't believe he did it!" Noah exclaimed.

Dylan pretended to be all teary-eyed and proud. "Our boy's all grow'd up."

Turns out, the girl was totally into Walker. In fact, after a lengthy tongue-bath, she broke away, got up, and took Walker by the hand *into the bedroom.*

Walker looked back at Dylan and Noah in sheer amazement. *How could it be that easy?* Dylan and Noah nodded their support and encouragement.

None of the smokers seemed to care one way or the other about the girl and Walker. The door closed and Noah turned to Dylan. "I wonder what Sarah's up to right now."

"Probably blowing some dude," Dylan chastised him for asking.

"Fuck you."

"I'm just kidding," Dylan pulled back. "Come on. We're in a super awesome drug den, there's a dead dude in the corner, and all you can think about is Sarah?"

"I really love her." Noah was feeling vulnerable and Dylan knew not to take advantage of it any further. It was his job to cheer Noah up.

"You say that now that you're broken up, but two weeks ago you were begging me to help you dump her."

"We had a fight."

"Look, man, I don't have any stake in this. I just want you to be happy."

Noah thanked him with a little nod and Dylan tried to change the subject. "Now can we please just be irresponsible while we still can?"

Noah looked at Dylan for a second, then smiled and went over to the couch to take a turn with the joint.

"Yes! That's what I'm talking about!" Dylan said to himself as he went over to join them.

In the tiny bedroom with only a mattress on the floor, a cheap particle-board dresser, and a picture of Jesus on the wall (Jesus Christ, not Jesus the drug dealer), Walker and the girl were making out.

"You have really nice eyes," Walker felt the need to say.

The girl smiled and in one motion pulled off her top. Walker's eyes went wide at seeing her black, lacy bra but he quickly contained his excitement and played it cool. Walker took off his own shirt.

"You are so hot. My name's Walker by the way."

She just smiled and pulled him onto the bed.

Back on the couch, Pike passed the joint to Jesus. Dylan noticed the case of brand new fire extinguishers stacked by the window. "Hey, what's with all the fire extinguishers?"

"Found 'em," said the fat guy, a man of apparently few words.

"Can we fuck around with them?" Dylan inquired.

The guy just shrugged.

Dylan went over, took one out, and pulled the pin. He pointed it at Pike's face and, without even saying a word, *pulled the trigger*.

Dylan blasted him with white foam, covering Pike's face like he got hit with a pie from an old Three Stooges movie.

Pike leapt up off the couch, beyond irate. "What the fuck!!!"

Everyone else just stared for a moment, then burst out laughing.

Things between Walker and the hot, stoned girl were progressing nicely. They were making out on the bed while Walker felt her up. Walker wasn't as hopeless as the guys thought—turns out, he was pretty skilled up to, and including, second base. His roaming hand undid her bra clasp and she helped him take her bra off altogether. Her breasts were something to behold. Small, but perfectly shaped and perky.

Maybe it was the pace at which things were progressing. Maybe it was the excitement of hooking up with a total stranger. Or maybe it was just that Walker knew he really was going to score this time. Whatever the reason, Walker suddenly felt the need to confess: "I should tell you, I've never done this before. So I might not be that good. I mean, I don't really know. Maybe I will be good at it. I've certainly thought about it a lot, but you know, just in case it's not good, that's why. Bottom line, though, if you just give me a chance, I'll try really hard."

The girl just stared at him blankly. He couldn't read her expression but it certainly seemed like maybe he just blew it.

After a moment, she finally spoke: "Lo siento. No hablo inglés."

Walker stared at her in disbelief. "You don't understand me."

He was dazed for a second. His whole ridiculous speech a moment ago hadn't turned her off. For all she knew, he was describing the various ways he was going to defile her. Whatever she might have thought he said, it didn't seem to turn her off the idea of having sex with him. To the contrary, she pulled a condom out of her purse and handed to him.

Walker just stared at her. She was so hot with her tight, naked body. This was the moment he'd dreamt of since he got hair on his balls. All he had to do was let it happen. But Walker was Walker, and Walker made everything complicated.

He stared at the condom, then back at her. Then, after what seemed like an eternity, he said, "I can't."

He sat up in bed.

She was confused.

"I'm sorry. You are very beautiful. This just isn't— It's not what I imagined."

She wondered what she had done wrong.

Walker continued, "I know you don't understand a word I'm saying but I just want my first time to be with someone I care about. I don't even know your name and you don't speak English so it's not like we're getting to know each other here. Ah, I'm such an idiot. Look, I appreciate the offer, but I just can't. I'm so sorry."

Walker pulled his shirt back on. Maybe she had no idea what had just happened, but at least she understood that they were done fooling around.

She gave Walker a reassuring hug before getting dressed.

The other room was now covered in foam from the fire extinguishers, and everyone was laughing like it was the funniest thing they'd ever seen.

Pike was on a swivel desk chair and propelled himself across the room by discharging the fire extinguisher. "Ev-a!" he screamed, doing his best Wall-e impersonation.

Just then, Walker emerged from the bedroom. His friends saw him and hooted and hollered. Walker couldn't help but blush. He made his way over to the couch and Dylan high-fived him.

"How was it?"

Walker was not about to tell them the truth, for fear of permanently obliterating his already pathetic sexual reputation. "Good. Awesome."

Dylan seemed more excited than Walker. "Yeah, baby!"

Noah patted Walker on the back. "She is so hot. Nicely done."

Walker tried to hide his embarrassment by changing the subject. "So let's head out."

Pike wasn't going anywhere. "We're fucking around with fire extinguishers."

Walker raised his voice, irritated. "So you guys want to stay here all night?"

Dylan picked up on the shift in Walker's demeanor and sensed something was up. He looked over at the girl still standing in the doorway with her arms crossed. He knew what girls looked like after sex, and that wasn't it.

He covered for Walker, "Yeah, Walker's right. Let's get going."

The others agreed and Pike packed up his book bag of weed.

Jesus opened the door and shook Pike's hand. "Say hi to Ned for me."

"Hey, where do you know Ned from anyway?" Dylan wondered aloud.

"Junior Entrepreneurs Camp."

Noah and Dylan looked at each other, amused.

As the guys headed out, Walker looked back at the girl one more time. They made eye contact and she smiled a goodbye.

Walker didn't regret his decision.

Jesus closed the door and walked back into the apartment. He turned to his cousin, Carmelita, and teasingly asked in Spanish, "You have fun, you big slut?"

Carmelita replied in Spanish, "Oh, nothing happened. He couldn't get it up."

CHAPTER ELEVEN

IT WAS CLOSE to nine p.m. and it was finally time to find the party Dylan kept talking about. They had paid eighty bucks each upfront and got special hologram-etched wristbands overnighted to them from Dylan's friend. It wasn't just supposed to be *better* than a high school party, it was supposed to be in a whole other category, and the guys were starting to get really excited.

Dylan drove south on the West End Highway as Noah read the text message off Dylan's phone. Walker was checking for GPS directions on Pike's phone but for some reason the address didn't seem to exist, which kind of made the party seem even cooler.

"It says it's off Front Street," Noah told the others.

"I'm freaking hungry," Pike moaned, his munchies kicking in. "Can we stop for some food?"

Walker found something on Pike's phone. "This says Front Street is near Wall Street."

Noah wasn't sure. "The warehouse is near Wall Street? That can't be right."

"Let's just ask for directions," Walker suggested.

But Dylan felt confident that the warehouse would magically reveal itself to them. "Relax. We'll find it."

Forty minutes later, Dylan turned down Water Street for the third time. They were officially lost. They tried turning onto Fulton Street, then Beekman.

Thirty minutes after that, they were completely off target, cruising up Avenue A.

"Is this the Village?" Noah asked. Sure, West Hartford was only two hours away from New York, but that didn't make them any more familiar with the streets than an average tourist.

"I'm hungry!" Pike repeated for the millionth time.

"Just ask for directions," Walker harped once again.

Dylan was losing his cool. "I don't need directions. We're almost there."

They stopped at a red light. Walker took the initiative by rolling down his window and yelling over to a cute young woman, "Hey, do you know where Front Street is?"

She came over and leaned in through the window. On closer inspection, the guys saw that she was obviously a street walker. If you couldn't tell by the cheap blonde wig, then maybe the fishnet stockings and pink halter-top might have given it away.

She looked around the car and eyed the four guys. "Sure, I know where it is," she replied, then smiled at Walker. "Do you need a date?"

"Sure!" Walker blurted out without thinking.

And with that, she opened the door and got in.

Noah turned back to Walker. "Are you kidding me?"

But Walker just looked clueless as usual. "What?"

"Dude, she's a hooker," Pike explained.

"No, she's not," Walker shrugged off.

"Pretty sure..." Pike shot back.

The prostitute just looked at them, confused. She could obviously hear this whole conversation.

The light changed and Dylan had no choice but to continue up Avenue A. He just shook his head, wondering how Walker ever got into college.

And the hooker now started to wonder what the hell was going on. She turned to Walker and asked, "So do you want me to suck you off or what?"

Without turning around, Dylan shouted to the back seat, "Yes, that would be fantastic. But first, my friend Walker there would like to know how much *money* it would cost to engage in the aforementioned sex act."

"Dylan!" Walker yelled, still clinging to the belief that this woman was just a nice girl. Perhaps a bit fashion-challenged, and obviously promiscuous, but not a prostitute! He felt embarrassed that Dylan was insulting her.

But the hooker merely sensed an opportunity and replied, "For three hundred I'll blow all four of you."

And that's when Walker finally realized his error and turned bright red.

"No, thanks," Pike answered matter-of-factly. "I think I got AIDS from a homeless guy's poop."

Walker was thoroughly humiliated and tried to explain, "I'm sorry. I really thought you wanted to go on a date with me."

"You think this is funny? I got rent to pay." She started to get agitated.

Walker tried to calm her down. "No, honestly, we're going to a party and I thought you wanted to go with me."

"Fine. I'll go with you for a hundred dollars. And I'll throw in a hand job."

Dylan finally ended the suffering with: "Walker, just give her twenty bucks for being a moron."

Walker sucked it up, pulled out his wallet, and handed her a twenty.

Dylan pulled over to the curb. "Sorry for wasting your time."

She rolled her eyes, opened the door, and got out… right in front of a police officer.

The officer wasn't even paying attention, but Walker panicked and blurted out, "She's not a prostitute."

That succeeded in getting the cop's attention. The police officer leaned his head into the car. "Excuse me?"

The other guys shrank in embarrassment.

"She's my date," Walker nervously lied. "We're going to a graduation party."

"I see," said the cop.

Dylan smiled at the cop, pointed with his thumb at Walker in the back seat, and whispered proudly, "He's going to Brandeis next year."

The officer looked the guys over, then closed Walker's door for him, patted the roof of the car, and sent them on their way. "Drive safe, boys." Then he turned to the prostitute and said, "And you be safe, too, Coco."

Dylan pulled out into traffic and turned left onto Houston Street.

Walker, still embarrassed, mumbled, "It was an honest mistake."

Dylan shouted into the back seat, "Will you two fuckheads stay away from all the hookers and con men please?"

"I found the queen the first two times!"

"We're almost at the Brooklyn Bridge," Dylan noted. "You want me to see if it's still for sale?"

Noah laughed and changed the subject. "Look, it's still early. Let's just find some place to hang out."

"And get some food!" Pike reminded them.

"We can ask for directions or get a new map or whatever," Walker tried to convince Dylan. "But I'm tired of driving around in circles."

"Okay, okay," Dylan gave in to the majority will, then added under his breath, "What a bunch of girls."

Dylan parked on Bleecker Street in the heart of Greenwich Village. They all got out and Dylan said, "Everyone remember where we parked."

The Cube beeped locked and they headed out.

The guys walked around for a bit to get the lay of the land, and soon the guys found themselves on MacDougal Street. Greenwich Village was a fun part of Manhattan that the guys had never really explored on previous trips into the city with their parents. It didn't have as many desperate weirdos as the East Village, but it was still a lot more eclectic than back home. NYU students, young gay men, and visiting hipsters crowded the narrow streets filled with cool beer halls, funky clothes stores, and trendy cafés. The warm weather really brought people outside and the fun vibe of cool, young people everywhere was intoxicating. It felt like no matter which way they turned, something was *happening*. It was like a music festival. Or Spring Break in Cabo… at least according to MTV.

Suddenly, Dylan announced, "Two o'clock, check it out."

It was a group of five super-hot girls their age.

"Let's see where they're heading," Dylan suggested, and immediately changed directions to intercept them.

"No, come on," Pike whined. "You said we were gonna eat. I'm starving."

"You've just got the munchies," Noah said dismissively.

But Walker took Pike's side in this debate, saying, "I could eat."

"Fine," Dylan replied quickly, keeping his eyes on the girls. "Go grab something. We'll meet up with you later. I'll text you where we are."

"Cool," Pike agreed and he headed out with Walker to find some food.

Dylan turned to Noah, happy to be temporarily free of the dead weight of Pike and Walker. They were great to have around 99% of the time, but when it came to stalking prey you needed to travel light, and one wingman was plenty. "Come on."

Dylan started running after the group of girls and Noah ran to catch up. As he got within shouting distance, Dylan slowed down and got their attention. "Hey! Hey."

The girls stopped and turned around. They looked roughly eighteen, dressed a bit fancy, and seemed rich. Dylan guessed they were from Manhattan or maybe Long Island. Either way, he could tell just from looking that these girls were up for some fun, and it was actually a lot easier to convince five girls to get crazy than just one or two.

Noah let Dylan take the lead, of course, and Dylan didn't let him down. "Hey, I'm Dylan," he began. "Listen. We are totally lost. We were supposed to meet some friends but we're not from the city. Can you help us out?"

The girls looked them over.

Leah, the cute one with short brown hair that fell over her eyes, answered. "Where are you supposed to meet them?"

"Where are you guys going?" Dylan avoided a direct answer.

Becky, the tall one with the long hair, said, "Element."

"That's the name of the place," Dylan continued fabricating. He turned to Noah and asked, "Element, right?" for added credibility.

Noah played along. "Yeah, I'm pretty sure that sounds right."

Dylan smiled and waited. He knew that's all he had to do.

Finally, the first one, Leah, suggested, "Do you want to come with us?"

But Dylan surprisingly played it coy. "I don't know. Our girlfriends might get jealous."

Noah looked at Dylan like he was crazy, but Dylan knew exactly what he was doing. First, by mentioning that they had girlfriends, Dylan had conveyed that they were into girls, but just not them, and were therefore safe to hang out with. But second, by playing it coy, the girls wanted them even more because, according to Dylan, girls always want what they can't have.

Leah played right into his hand and replied, "Don't worry. We won't molest you."

The girls laughed and Leah took Dylan by the arm. Becky linked arms with wild looking Chelsea, buxom blonde Faith, and waspy looking Caitlin. Together, the four girls grabbed Noah and escorted him down the street as well.

CHAPTER TWELVE

PIKE AND WALKER made their way down to Chinatown. They could have been eating by now but Pike was a surprisingly picky eater for someone who was perpetually hungry.

Walker spotted a sign in one window. "There, there you go. All you can eat, nine ninety five."

Pike finally agreed. "Challenge accepted, Hop Li Buffet Restaurant." They headed in.

Soon, Walker and Pike were filling up their plates with food from the buffet in this Chinese restaurant with dead ducks hanging in the window. Walker was surprised at how busy the place was at this hour, but Pike explained that New York City was "like its own time zone." There were a lot of couples on dates and quite a few college kids who looked like they had the munchies worse than Pike.

They moved forward in the buffet line and Pike elbowed Walker. "Go for the shrimp. Pound for pound it's the most expensive thing here."

"I don't want shrimp." Walker scooped a mound of white rice instead.

Pike looked personally offended. "Dude, what the fuck are you doing? Rice costs like a nickel and it will fill you up before you get your money's worth."

A woman in front of them glanced back at Pike like he was an incredible asshole.

Walker rolled his eyes. "How am I supposed to eat Chinese food without rice? This is dinner, not an arbitrage opportunity." He scooped more rice onto his plate, defiantly.

Pike shrugged. "Whatever. Sucker."

───────

At Element, hundreds of people were dancing to the thumping techno music in this former 19th century bank, now an all-ages dance club. The place was huge, with three levels: the candlelit brick walls of the private mezzanine, the lower "vault" level with old-fashioned safe doors, and the main dance floor with its 36,000-watt sound system. Element was the kind of place that spent a lot of money telling the world how cool it was, which of course made it fairly *un*cool, but the girls picked the place, and Dylan would have followed them to the Post Office if he thought he might get lucky.

The crowd was mostly "bridge and tunnel"—few locals took Element seriously—but there were a lot of out-of-towners in the city tonight and the dance floor was packed. The silver lining was that Dylan could dance right up against Leah without the usual break-in period.

Leah was incredibly sexy. She had short hair almost like a boy's, but it fell over her green eyes like a picture you'd see in a hair salon. (Her haircut was actually very similar to Dylan's vision-obscuring do, and if Noah had been a Freudian psychologist, he might have suggested it was the reason Dylan was so into her.) She was wearing a low-cut black dress that barely covered her butt. The music was a nondescript bass line that they could feel in their teeth, but Leah seemed into it, so Dylan was into it as well.

Noah played the good wingman, keeping the other four girls occupied at the juice bar. He sipped his twelve dollar orange juice, then yelled to be heard, "Do you guys live here in Manhattan?"

Faith answered, "No, we just came in from the Island for the weekend."

Faith was stunning. She had long, curly blonde hair and piercing blue eyes. Her red dress was longer than Leah's—everyone's was—but on her, it just looked elegant. Noah could see she had some seriously big boobs packed in there but he tried his best not to let her catch him staring.

She added, "Leah's dad got her a suite at the Plaza for a graduation present."

Noah perked up. "Oh, you graduated this week? Our graduation is next week."

Chelsea nodded along. "Cool."

Chelsea had a possessed look in her eye. Noah would easily have guessed that she was the wild one, the instigator of all that was illegal, immoral, or just ill-conceived. She had wavy black hair, brown eyes, and a rocking, tight, athletic body. Maybe she wasn't as hot as Leah or as beautiful as Faith, but Noah imagined she made up for it in the sack.

Becky downed her cranberry juice and slammed the empty glass on the bar. "This place fucking sucks," she announced to no one in particular. Becky was the tallest, with long, brown hair and bangs. She was the only one with obvious tattoos, a Celtic arm-band on her left bicep and a series of Chinese symbols across the back of her shoulder blades. Noah figured the symbols meant something lame like "harmony," but frankly he didn't really care and wasn't going to ask.

"We should have just gone to a real bar," she lamented.

"Hey, but where else can you get a full day's supply of vitamin C for only twelve bucks?" Noah joked.

The girls laughed. But Caitlin was sick of the small talk and grabbed Noah's hand. "Come on, let's dance."

Caitlin had straight, blonde hair in a preppy bob. Her tight plaid miniskirt made her look like a Catholic schoolgirl, but her face said wasp all the way. Something about her Anglican nose, or her thin lips that rose into a natural smirk, made her seem full of herself. She wouldn't have been Noah's first choice—he probably would have gone for Faith or Chelsea—but she was the one dragging him onto the dance floor.

Sure, Noah was still thinking about Sarah in that moment, but this was Noah, not Walker, and *he* didn't need someone to push him into the arms of a gorgeous girl. Besides, he and Sarah *were* broken up.

Noah followed Caitlin through the crowd until they found a small space to start dancing. Caitlin was one of those girls who just really liked *dancing*, and Noah, it seemed, was there as more of an accessory. Sure enough, Becky, Chelsea, and Faith soon made their way over to join them and it quickly turned into more of a platonic group thing than a prelude to hooking up.

Dylan, on the other hand, was really putting the moves on Leah, grinding her on the dance floor and squeezing her ass. Not that she minded one bit. After all, Dylan was charming, good looking, and frankly, sexy, and he excelled at making girls feel good about doing what he wanted.

After a couple more songs, Dylan could tell he was working her into a frenzy.

Suddenly, Leah spotted her friends just a few yards away and yelled to them, "I'm starting to get sober. Let's go back to the Plaza."

Dylan, fearing he'd somehow blown it, asked, "Already? It's early."

Leah looked up into Dylan's eyes and asked innocently, "Do you guys want to come with us?"

Dylan smiled, amused that he had doubted himself even for a second. Noah and the girls worked their way over to Dylan and Leah. Dylan looked at Noah knowingly.

Before they knew it, Dylan and Noah found themselves in Leah's stretch limo, piled in with the five girls. All of them were laughing and sticking their heads out of the windows and sunroof.

The limo driver just rolled his eyes.

But Noah and Dylan didn't care. They had five hot, sexy, almost certainly promiscuous girls on their laps.

Walker and Pike chowed down, Pike on mostly shrimp and Walker on mostly rice. Between bites, Walker asked, "What do you think everyone's doing right now at Marco's beach house?"

"Who the fuck cares?" Pike snapped. "Live in the fucking moment, man." He took a big mouthful of Kung Pao Shrimp.

Walker sighed, then just kind of blurted out, "God, I need to get laid."

"Wait. I thought you just *got* laid. What about that girl?"

Oops.

Walker tried to cover. "Yeah, I mean I need to get laid *again*."

But Pike knew Walker too well. "You didn't do it, did you?"

Busted.

Walker blushed. "No."

Then, much to Walker's surprise, Pike demonstrated a rare moment of empathy when he said, "Hey, no worries, man. It'll happen."

Walker opened up. "I just couldn't. I mean, I didn't even know her name."

"Don't overthink it. Look at Dylan. If he thinks there's a chance a girl *won't* kick him in the balls, he just goes in for the kill. No chit chat, no baking lasagna, it's like a fucking surgical strike."

"Well, I'm not like that. Dylan told me I'm the kind of guy girls appreciate when they're older."

"Yeah, and Dylan told me to stop smoking so much pot."

Walker put down his fork. "I don't know. I feel like it's important to be friends first."

"How's that working out for you?" Pike laughed before letting out a tremendous burp. So much for the empathetic moment. He threw down his fork as well. "Man, I am stuffed."

"Me, too."

"Come on. Let's get some more food."

Walker was confused. "But you just said—"

Pike explained, "One more plate and we come out ahead."

"That's not nice. These people need to make a living."

Pike pretended to cry, complete with over-exaggerated boo hoo tear wiping.

But Walker put his foot down. "I'm sorry. I'm not wasting food on purpose."

"Fine. What a killjoy."

So instead of going back to the buffet, the two took the bill up to the cashier, an elderly Chinese lady who recited from memory, "Two buffet, plus tax, twenty-one fifty-seven."

Pike corrected her. "Oh, I didn't eat."

Walker flinched. *What the hell is Pike up to now?* He had that look in his eye.

The cashier was confused. "What you mean?"

Pike calmly explained, "He had the buffet, but I didn't eat. I was just keeping him company."

Walker was now in full-on panic mode. He was turning red, but of course he couldn't say anything. He was just frozen there watching it unfold before him.

The cashier challenged Pike. "You ate. I saw you eat."

Pike was confident. "No, you didn't. I didn't eat."

The cashier looked at Pike suspiciously, then shouted out something in Chinese. A busboy came over and they argued loudly in Chinese.

Walker would have done anything in the world to get the hell out of there. He pulled out his money. "I ate a lot. Maybe I'll just pay for two—"

But Pike stopped him. "No way. You're not paying for me if I didn't eat."

The cashier argued some more with the busboy and became increasingly angry with him. After some time, the busboy, sufficiently chewed out, bowed and trudged away.

The cashier was pissed. The busboy must not have been able to of-fer any concrete proof on the controversy because the cashier just glared at Pike and said, "Okay. One buffet. Ten seventy-eight."

Walker quickly peeled off a ten and a five and muttered, "Keep the change," before hightailing it out of there with Pike.

Once outside, Pike started laughing his ass off but Walker was livid. "What the fuck was that?!"

"What?"

"We could have gotten arrested! Or worse! They could have been Triads!"

"Or ninjas!" Pike shot back. "You know, you worry too much." He laughed.

"Come on," Pike changed the subject, "let's check in." He reached for his cell phone but it wasn't in his pocket. He checked his other pockets. Then Pike's face went white.

"You have my cell?"

"No."

Pike patted himself down. "Fuck me. I left it on the table."

Walker saw he was serious and immediately burst out laughing.

"Ha ha, very funny," Pike snarled.

Walker did the proverbial "answering the phone" motion with his hand. "Hello? Yeah, it's karma calling. It wants to laugh its ass off in your face."

But Pike was no longer in a mood for jokes. "Go in and get it," he ordered.

"Uh uh. No way. Ditch meet digger. You get your own phone."

Pike knew Walker would never go back in there for all the tea in China, so to speak. "Fine," he said, and went back in.

Pike locked eyes with the cashier but didn't stop, walking right past her to the table. But it had been cleared. No cell phone.

Pike spotted the busboy who had been chewed out and stopped him. "Hey, man. Did you see a cell phone? I left it on the table."

The busboy barely spoke English and replied merely, "No phone."

"Are you sure? It was a BlackBerry. Brand new? I left it right here on the table."

"No phone."

Pike crouched down and looked under the table. Not there.

He went over to the buffet table. No phone.

He went back to the cashier. He was going to ask her if she'd seen it, but when their eyes met once again, he thought better of it.

He walked out, dejected.

But as he was leaving, the cashier called out to him, "Next time, *phone* ahead, we give you best seat in the house."

Pike stopped and turned around. The old lady was smiling, ear to ear. They had his phone all right, but there wasn't a damn thing he could do about it.

He walked out.

Outside, Walker asked, "You find it?"

"No." Pike stamped his foot. "Fuck!"

Walker looked concerned. "How are we going to meet up with Dylan and Noah?"

"Well, if you had your own cell…" Pike chastised.

Walker reminded him, "My mom says I don't need one."

"And *that's* why you never get laid," Pike lashed out at Walker.

Walker was confused. "Because I don't have a cell phone?" He wondered whether that could possibly be true.

CHAPTER THIRTEEN

MEANWHILE, AT THE Plaza, Dylan, Noah, and the five girls took the elevator up to the nineteenth floor. They didn't talk much in the elevator; it was a slightly awkward moment where the guys didn't want to jinx anything and the girls just wanted to get another drink in them to refuel their desire to be bad.

The elevator door opened and Leah led them down the hall to 1915. She swiped her key card and walked in just ahead of Dylan.

The suite was huge, with two bedrooms, a master bathroom suite, and a living room with a separate bar area. The Louis XV décor looked like it was from out of a Marie Antoinette movie. There were exquisite chairs, an antique writing desk, and sofas even the tidiest adult would be afraid to sit on. Dylan had no idea what a room like this cost but he knew it would be described as "a shitload."

"Jesus, pretty nice graduation present. What's your dad do?"

"Hedge funds," Leah scoffed derisively. In just those two words Dylan knew she had daddy issues, and girls with daddy issues always sought to resolve those issues with Dylan. Between the sheets.

The girls headed straight for the bar. There was already a nice collection of half-empty bottles of vodka and rum on the counter, along with sodas and other mixers. The sumptuous accommodations apparently hadn't deterred the girls from trashing the place. It was a mess, with clothes and shopping bags from Bloomingdales and Saks strewn all over the sitting area. Half-eaten room service still sat on the serving cart in the entryway, and there were liquor bottles everywhere. These girls were hard-partiers, and it occurred to Noah that maybe they were a little *too* degenerate, even if they were super hot. Noah had never felt like a yokel before until now.

Becky prodded her friends along. "Come on. Let's get fucked up." She poured a rum and Diet Coke into a crystal glass and drank half of it in one swig.

Chelsea had a crazy look in her eyes. She took out a bottle of prescription pills from her purse and unabashedly popped one down with a vodka chaser.

Dylan looked at Noah, grinning ear to ear. This was going to be too easy.

But Noah did not see these girls as simple prey; he was starting to get conflicted. He pulled Dylan aside. "Are you sure about this?"

Dylan wasn't sure if Noah was pining for Sarah, freaked out by the quantity of booze and drugs, or just upset by the speed at which it all was going down, but Dylan knew it was now his job to ease Noah's conscience.

"Listen to me. Do not blow this or it will haunt you for the rest of your days!"

"But—"

Dylan grabbed him by the shoulders and actually shook him. "Let. This. Happen."

Noah realized the debate was over, and it wouldn't hurt to be a little more adventurous. And who knows? This probably *would* turn out pretty memorably.

"Okay, okay."

Pike and Walker walked down Canal Street trying to figure out how to get back in touch with Dylan and Noah without a cell phone. *How did people meet up with each other in the olden days?*, they wondered.

"Let's just try to find them back in the Village," Pike suggested.

Walker scoffed. "Yeah, good idea. New York's pretty small."

Pike frowned, seeing Walker's point. Pretty unlikely to just magically run into Dylan and Noah in a city of thirteen million, compared to West Hartford where it happened all the time. Hell, in middle school, Pike used to just go to Bishop's Corner and hang out in front of the drugstore until somebody from school walked by with an idea on how to pass the time.

Walker saw something. "Look."

There, a little bit down the street was... a *pay phone*.

They walked up to it.

Pike stared at it for a moment. "How does it work?" he asked, as if it were a sextant.

"Don't be an idiot," Walker chastised.

Pike picked up the receiver and dialed Dylan's cell number. He listened, unsure of whether this was going to work or not. Then he pulled the phone away from his ear and reported to Walker, "It says it's long distance. How can that be right? He's got to be within a couple of miles of here."

Walker rolled his eyes. "Are you retarded?"

Walker grabbed the phone from him, hung up, and dialed again. He listened to the recording and explained, "We need a dollar seventy. Do you have any change?"

"No. I've only got twenties."

"Maybe we can get change in there," Walker suggested, indicating an all-night laundromat.

Pike shrugged and Walker hung up the phone.

In the laundromat, Pike and Walker spied a change machine. Pike put a twenty in and out poured a pile of quarters.

Walker shook his head. "Idiot, we don't need twenty bucks worth of quarters."

"I told you, I've only got twenties."

"Well, I'm not carrying around ten pounds of quarters."

It was odd. With all the guys, Walker was usually low man on the totem pole. He took a lot of shit for being pathetic with women, but he didn't mind because deep down he kind of agreed with them. But around Pike, Walker was often in charge. Pike was, after all, kind of dumb, at least compared to Walker. And Pike was usually not possessed of great common sense, even when he wasn't stoned.

Pike scooped up the quarters with two hands and looked around for a way to change them back into bills. Over in the corner was a cute older girl in her twenties waiting for her laundry. She was wearing a tie-dye t-shirt and reading Camus' *A Happy Death*. Pike forgot about the quarters. He was usually fueled by impulses and one had just fired in his pants.

He turned to Walker. "I'll take care of these. You go call Dylan." He handed Walker some of the quarters and Walker rolled his eyes before heading out.

Returning to the pay phone, Walker dropped a quarter in the slot, but for some reason the phone just spit it out into the coin return. Walker tried again. Same result. He stared at the payphone for a moment, a little embarrassed that he couldn't figure out how to use it. But then again, Walker had literally never used a payphone before. He picked up the receiver and actually read the instructions printed on the phone. This time he dialed first. He deposited the quarters as instructed and the line started ringing.

Dylan's cell phone was sitting on the couch in the suite at the Plaza, ringing with the ringtone version of Cake's "Short Skirt/Long Jacket." Unfortunately, there was no one there to answer it.

Next to the cell phone was Dylan's shirt. On the floor, Noah's jeans. Miniskirts and high heels led directly to the adjacent room where loud laughter and fun-sounding shrieks were coming from the bathroom.

Inside the master bathroom suite were Dylan, Noah, and all five girls *in the massive Jacuzzi bathtub*, laughing, drinking, and splashing around with the Jacuzzi jets blasting. A bottle of tequila rested precariously on the edge of the tub, and the iPod dock was pumping out some lame pop song the guys had never heard of.

The girls were in bras and panties, the guys in their boxers, and they were playing "Truth or Dare." Up until this point, the dares had been fairly tame—Caitlin flashed her tits, Dylan did a rum shot out of Leah's belly button—and the truths even tamer. But the girls were getting more and more wasted (especially Chelsea, whose eyes were starting to roll back), and they were ready to take the party to the next level.

Becky looked at Leah. "Your turn."

Leah laughed. "Okay, okay. Dare."

Faith quickly issued the challenge, "I dare you to go into the bedroom with Dylan."

The girls all ooh'ed and giggled. Dylan raised an eyebrow to Noah. Whatever these girls needed to tell themselves to make it all okay was fine with him.

Leah looked at Dylan as she had been doing all night long, like a girl who knew what she wanted. "Okay, I'll do it," she giggled, as if there were any doubt.

More laughing. More splashing. Noah took a swig of tequila.

Leah stepped out of the bathtub, her wet underwear practically see-through. She had a great body with only a hint of baby fat, and her ass glistened as the water ran off of it. She took Dylan by the hand and he got out as well. Leah escorted Dylan into the master bedroom amid the chorus of cheers from the other four girls.

And that left Noah in a sea of cute, wet, drunk girls.

The game continued. "Your turn, Chelsea," Caitlin chirped. There didn't seem to be any real order as to whose turn it was, and Noah wondered if the girls had somehow worked all this out between themselves without the guys knowing.

"Truth," Chelsea said, as her eyes drooped. She was by far the most fucked up of the girls, and Noah made a mental note that no matter what happened he wouldn't let her be alone in the bathtub. All he needed was a dead girl with a .28 blood alcohol content and a stomach full of pills to find its way onto his high school transcript. Chelsea was cute, with her curly black hair and six-pack abs, but you wouldn't want to sell her life insurance. If she made it out of college alive, it'd be a miracle.

Faith bounced up and down, "I've got it. I've got it." She was the blonde with the large rack, and Noah couldn't help watch her mesmerizing bosom heave under the thin layer of a black bra. She saw Noah staring and didn't care. She just smiled and turned back to Chelsea, asking, "Have you ever videotaped yourself having sex?"

Noah laughed along with the other girls while Chelsea thought about it. She may have been unconscious—Noah wasn't sure—but after a moment, her eyes opened and she said "yes" with a maniacal laugh.

The girls burst out laughing.

"Jesus," Noah said, stunned.

Chelsea backtracked, slurring, "But wait, but wait. I can explain." Then after an unintentionally dramatic pause, she did in fact explain, "I was drunk."

The girls all burst out laughing again and Noah took another swig of tequila. He wondered if all the girls from the city or Long Island, or wherever they were from, were this nihilistic.

Becky, who Noah was starting to realize was the instigator of the group, turned to him and declared, "Okay, your turn."

Noah was equal parts psyched to see where this was going and scared that these girls might turn on a dime and stab him in the eye with an ice pick. But he figured the only way something good was going to happen was to take a chance.

"Okay. Dare."

The girls giggled.

Becky consulted her mental library of inter-gender bathtub dares and came up with, "I dare you to kiss Faith and Chelsea. At the same time."

Noah smiled. This was *not* a problem.

Chelsea and Faith looked at Becky innocently, on the surface appearing as though this would somehow push them past their normal comfort level, but Noah wasn't buying it. He could see these girls had obviously done shit like this before, and probably a lot worse.

Caitlin moved aside and Noah leaned over and kissed Faith on the lips. She was a good kisser, despite the taste of rum and coke and cigarettes. She stuck her tongue down his throat.

Chelsea waded over to him and jealously pulled his face away from Faith. Noah began French-kissing her and although she didn't taste much better, something about the way she grabbed the hair on the back of his head convinced Noah she'd be incredible in bed. Maybe there *was* life after Sarah after all.

Feeling left out, Faith got back into Noah's orbit and Noah began kissing them both at the same time. There was no way to do it other than full-on porno style, with their tongues lapping in mid-air. He glanced for a second at Becky who seemed really into watching, and Noah wondered if maybe she was into girls. Caitlin at least pretended to look away and took another drink of vodka. Noah's mind drifted back to the matter at hand: He was currently making out with two incredible, wet, sexy girls. It was probably the hottest thing Noah had ever done, or would ever do, in his lifetime.

After a good two or three minutes of the three of them playing tongue judo with each other, Becky grew restless. "Okay, guys," she interrupted, "I think your turn is up…" But Noah wasn't going anywhere. Not as long as these two girls were still willing to suck face with him, and more importantly, each other.

"This is so exactly like last weekend," Caitlin whispered to Becky, exasperated.

Noah smiled, his curiosity getting the best of him. He pulled away from the kiss just a fraction of an inch and gently asked, "What was last weekend?"

"Naomi Feldman's bat mitzvah at the Waldorf," Faith explained with a knowing look, obviously recalling some depraved incident.

But Becky flinched slightly and tried to cover by changing the subject. "Ooh, I love this song. Turn it up."

Caitlin turned up the volume on the iPod dock and Noah now noticed that it was, in fact, Justin Bieber. He cocked his head. *Who listens to Justin Bieber?* He played back the transcript in his mind and picked up on the slip-up.

Chelsea grabbed Noah's face and tried to kiss him again but Noah stopped her. "Wait, what were you doing at a bat mitzvah?" he asked Faith accusingly. "How old are you?"

"Fifteen," Faith lied.

That didn't make any sense and Noah knew it. "*How old are you*?!" he repeated.

Faith lowered her head in shame. "Thirteen." She looked at Becky guiltily, sorry for blowing it. Becky just rolled her eyes.

Noah, on the other hand, felt violated. "You said this was a graduation present!"

"Yeah. From junior high," Caitlin admitted.

That's all Noah needed to hear. He bolted out of the bathtub and searched frantically for a towel.

Becky tried to smooth things over. "Come on. Don't go," she pleaded. "We were having a good time."

But Noah was livid. When you're eighteen, a high school senior, and about to go off to college—Brown, no less—you don't make out with eighth graders, no matter how hot, promiscuous, or degenerate they might be. It was just creepy.

Noah was desperately trying to get the hell out of there but the bathroom was a pig sty, with girls clothes strewn everywhere and make-up and hair products littering the counters. "Where the hell are my clothes?!"

In the elegantly appointed master bedroom, Dylan and Leah were making out under the sheets. He had long ago gotten her out of her wet bra and panties (she hadn't raised any objections) and they were really getting into things.

Dylan didn't need to ask if she was ready. He just reached for his jeans and pulled out a condom. Leah smiled and Dylan put it on under the sheets. But as he got on top of her, about to put it in, she suddenly looked surprised and said, "Wait, wait. Stop."

Dylan froze.

"I can't do that."

"You can't?" Dylan replied, confused. That was the *last* thing he'd expected to hear.

"I'm a vaginal virgin," she admitted.

"A what?" he blurted out. He honestly had no idea what she was talking about.

"I'm waiting till marriage," she explained.

"Seriously?"

This whole thing was getting weirder and weirder. Never in a million years would Dylan have guessed she was a virgin, let alone one waiting till marriage. Hell, Leah didn't seem like she waited for a name.

But she reassured him. "Don't worry. We can still do it."

Now Dylan was totally baffled. "We can?"

She laughed. "Yeah, of course. Just not there."

But before Dylan could confirm what "vaginal virgin" meant, Noah burst into the room.

"Ocupado!" Dylan barked.

But Noah was not leaving alone and he *was* leaving. "Come on, let's get out of here." He threw Dylan's pants at him. Leah pulled the covers up to her chin and the other girls watched the drama from the doorway.

Dylan was more than a little annoyed. "What the fuck? I'm busy, dude. Is this payback for the other night?"

Noah dropped the bombshell. "Dylan, these girls are thirteen."

The proverbial record skipped.

Dylan, still on top of Leah in a sensual embrace, looked her in the eye. "You're thirteen?" he asked, desperately hoping this was some sort of joke.

Leah looked over at her friends in the doorway, and Becky nodded toward Faith as the one who had blown it. Leah knew the jig was up.

She looked up at Dylan innocently and said, "No, but I will be next month."

Twenty-three seconds later, Dylan and Noah were outside on Fifth Avenue, standing in front of the Plaza Hotel.

"I've got an idea." Dylan suggested. "Let's never mention this to anyone."

Noah knew this was Dylan's way of apologizing. He had pushed Noah into this fiasco every step of the way, and for once Noah felt vindicated. His Spidey-sense had been tingling and he should have trusted his instincts instead of listening to Dylan. But that was usually the nature of their relationship. Dylan knew it was hard to say no to him, and sometimes he abused that trust. Sure, he had wanted to make some memories this weekend, but this was not exactly what he was shooting for. So this was Dylan being contrite.

"That seems prudent," Noah replied, rubbing it in his face a bit.

They just looked at each other for a moment, then burst out laughing.

All was forgiven.

CHAPTER FOURTEEN

As DYLAN AND Noah walked down Fifth Avenue, Dylan dialed Pike's cell phone to check in but there was no answer. Instead, the busboy from Hop Li Buffet Restaurant, in the alley on a cigarette break, pressed ignore and tucked Pike's phone back into his shirt pocket.

"No answer," Dylan reported.

"Let's just head back to the car," Noah shrugged.

They headed into the subway station, bought some tokens, and studied the subway map. Concluding that the E train was the best bet to get back to the Village, they headed down to the platform and waited.

A train approached, but it was the C train. The guys stepped back and let the passengers get in and out. Then, as the doors closed, Noah spotted someone inside the train.

It was Sarah.

And what's more, she was with some Chace Crawford-looking dude.

"Sarah?" Noah blurted out, in disbelief.

Dylan turned and saw her as well, so he knew Noah wasn't crazy.

The car started to leave the station.

"Sarah!" Noah yelled.

Noah ran up to the car and pounded on the door, but it was no use. She didn't notice him and the train sped away.

Noah looked panicked. "What's Sarah doing here in the city?!" he asked frantically.

"And who's that dude?" Dylan added, indelicately.

Noah dug out his phone and starting dialing, but Dylan tried to talk him off the proverbial ledge. "What are you doing?"

"Calling her."

"Don't do that. Come on."

Dylan tried to take the phone away but Noah wouldn't let him. Noah dialed, listened for a moment, then looked back at his phone, cursing himself.

"No signal." Noah lashed out at Dylan: "Damn it! I shouldn't have listened to you! We should have just gone to Marco's!"

"That doesn't make any sense. Sarah isn't even at Marco's."

"Yeah, well, if I was at Marco's I wouldn't have seen her with that guy!"

"There you go. That's the spirit. Complete denial."

Noah looked helpless, and Dylan had run out of ideas to comfort him. So they just waited on the platform for their train.

At the laundromat, Walker was playing wingman while Pike chatted with Haley, the twenty-something girl in the tie-dye t-shirt.

Haley was pontificating about something, then paused dramatically. "I don't know, I guess I'm just a very spiritual person," she announced pretentiously.

Walker rolled his eyes. He hated girls who said they were "spiritual."
If they believed in God and went to church or temple or whatever, fine,
just say you're religious. But "spiritual" girls usually weren't religious at
all; they just believed in nonsensical crap like auras and Ouija boards.

But Pike was playing along and replied, "Me, too! You know, I
sensed that about you. I'm very intuitive about these things."

Walker wondered whether Pike would have been onboard with her
babble if she'd said she was a pedophile. Or a Nazi.

The dryer buzzed and Haley started collecting her clothes. "Hey, do
you guys want to head down to Soho to this amazing club where they
do performance art?"

"Yes. Yes, we do," Pike answered with a straight face.

"But what about Dylan and Noah?" Walker reminded him.

"We'll catch up with them later." Pike eyed Walker in the hopes that
he might be a little more agreeable.

Walker didn't want to be a cock-blocker, so he signed off with an
albeit unconvincing, "Okay. Sounds good."

Haley grabbed her basket of clothes and they headed out.

On the street, Haley gushed, "You guys are going to love this. Did
you ever see 'Interior Scroll' by Carolee Schneemann?"

The guys shook their heads no.

"It's amazing," Haley continued. "She unrolls a scroll from her vagina onstage and reads a speech written on it about sexism and meat."

"Sounds very powerful," Pike commented thoughtfully.

Walker looked at Pike, like, *What the hell are we getting into?*

After they dropped off Haley's laundry at her apartment, the three
of them took a taxi to "der Freiheitsgestalt" in the heart of Soho. It was

little more than a dark, dirty bar with a dozen small tables and an elevated stage you might see at an elementary school holiday pageant. The name was taken from the German performance artist Joseph Beuys' social sculpture movement in which he spent three days in 1974 in a room with a wild coyote. And Joseph Beuys would have been proud of the progress of history: Onstage, a naked man was giving a silent, seated Chinese woman a haircut. Literally.

As he cut five inches off the back, he melodramatically recited:

Potential life? Potential death.

Clone, hone, velodrome.

His dong flapped in the wind as he snipped off another large section of the woman's hair, giving her a bald patch on one side.

Pike and Walker sat with Haley at a table near the front. Walker stared blankly at the "artist" while Pike did his best to appear into it, nodding his head approvingly. Next to Pike, Haley snapped her applause (only troglodytes applaud by clapping with their hands).

She whispered to Pike, "This is so visceral."

The pot earlier in the evening must have made Pike really horny because even though Haley was a cute girl with curly brown hair, only a committed pussy-hound would sit through this crap. But Pike continued the grungy intellectual charade and played it for all it was worth, replying, "It's very raw."

"Exactly!" Haley gushed.

Walker spoke up, wondering aloud, "Does she get naked, too?"

Pike elbowed him.

Haley leaned over and whispered, "That's not a woman."

Confused, Walker strained to get a better look.

The naked guy cut another large section of hair, reciting:

Lenticular process? Follicular holocaust.

D.N.A., C.I.A., Chardonnay.

The audience snapped their approval.

Pike leaned over and whispered to Haley, "You wanna get baked?" No soul-searching, hand-wringing, or elaborate plans with Pike, just a spur-of-the-moment suggestion, a whim really.

Haley smiled. "You've got some?"

Sure, the brick of marijuana was in the back seat of the Cube, but Pike had remembered to pilfer a small supply off the top. He raised an eyebrow.

"My hero," she beamed.

She took his hand and they stood up.

Walker protested, "Wait, where are you going?" but they didn't answer. Walker watched helplessly as they abandoned him.

Onstage, the Chinese "woman" was losing more hair.

"Great," Walker muttered to himself.

CHAPTER FIFTEEN

DYLAN AND NOAH rode the E train downtown as Noah frantically surfed the web on his phone with an intermittent-at-best signal.

"There," he finally announced. "Thank you, Twitter."

He read Sarah's tweet: "'Heading down to Stark Raving Mad 2012.'" Noah was confused. "Wait. She's going to our party?"

"How did she find out about it?" Dylan asked, a tad annoyed that the party wasn't as exclusive as he thought.

"Probably from Gossip Girl back there."

"Hey, check, maybe he's one of her friends..."

Noah waited for his signal to come back, then started scanning through Sarah's list of Facebook friends. During a signal outage, Noah told Dylan, "We need to get to that party."

"What are you going to do? She's with that guy."

"I don't know, but I have to do something."

Dylan looked skeptical.

Noah found something. "There he is. Kim Striker." Noah looked up at Dylan. "Seriously? What kind of dumb name is that? He has a girl's name!" Noah was not taking the news of Sarah's apparent moving-on well.

Dylan grabbed the phone and looked at Kim Striker's profile. "He's a freshman at U. of W."

This was getting worse and worse for Noah. "She probably met him when she visited the school," he sighed. "Come on! How long does this train take?"

The truth was that Sarah *had* met Kim Striker at the University of Wisconsin when she was visiting Madison during her February break. He was a freshman and led the campus tour. They had hit it off right away—he was an art history major and that was something Sarah was seriously considering. After the tour, they exchanged emails.

Sarah hadn't thought much about it at the time. After all, she had a serious boyfriend and made that fact clear to anyone who perused her Facebook profile. So when Kim emailed her a couple of weeks later, she naturally assumed it was innocent, which it mostly was.

"Any other questions about the school, just give me a shout," was all he wrote. Sarah did have a few more questions—*Did everyone pretty much join a sorority or was it cool not to pledge? Can you change your major after you declare? Did Kim ever feel lost in such a big school?*—and Kim and Sarah became friends. In April, when Sarah found out she got in, Kim was the first person she told, even before Noah.

To Sarah, Kim was just a friend. Kim, however, had obviously considered the possibility that knowing a hot freshman girl might pay dividends in the Fall. There was little effort in maintaining the Facebook friendship, and Kim had seen how things change between girls and their "serious" boyfriends. Especially when the boyfriend is suddenly a thousand miles away and the girl is plopped down in a campus with 30,000 undergraduates. It was just a fact of life and it cost Kim nothing to wait and see.

So when Sarah called him suddenly last week—an actual phone call, not a text or email—crying about how she broke up with her boyfriend, Kim was glad she couldn't see his shit-eating grin. He consoled her for as long as he could stand it, then offered to cheer her up with a trip into the city. Kim was already out of school for the summer and had scored an awesome internship at the MOMA. Another intern that he was hooking up with had told him about Stark Raving Mad and after a few texts, he had two wristbands.

The ironic thing was that Sarah only agreed to go into New York to see Kim because she thought Noah was going to be at Marco's house. She just didn't think she could deal with seeing Noah all weekend long. So Sarah lied to her parents and took the train into Grand Central by herself.

Kim met her by the clock with a big hug. Sarah hadn't really thought of Kim in that way before, but after talking to him the other night and seeing him now, she couldn't help but wonder if something might happen between them on this visit.

Kim took her to the theater district to get Ethiopian food (which Sarah had never had before). Then they went back to Kim's sublet on the Upper West Side that he shared with five other guys from Madison. After a million questions about the school, and some obscene *Are you going to bone her?* gestures behind her back, Sarah stowed her stuff and changed to go out.

Sarah wasn't sure she was ready to move on just yet. She felt a pang of guilt about even being on this trip. Even though she and Noah were over, they had been a couple for a long time and they were in love, for Christ's sake. You don't just move on to some other guy after one week. But all her friends told her she was crazy not to go off with a hot college guy like Kim Striker, so she did it.

They took the C train downtown together, listening on split headphones to Kim's iPod. He was playing some band Sarah had never heard of before called "Vivian Girls." But it was good and Sarah looked over at Kim and they shared a smile. It occurred to her that sitting with Kim on the subway just kicking back and listening to music like this was actually kind of romantic. She didn't know where things were going to wind up tonight, but part of her decided then and there that it would be good for her to go off to college with a little more sexual experience.

Noah was inconsolable. All he wanted to do now was get to the damn party and talk to Sarah. They made their way from Washington Square Station to Bleecker Street where the car was parked.

Only there was no car.

Dylan looked up and down the street. There were no cars parked on this side. He looked at the signs and concluded, "This is a tow zone."

"No, it's not," Noah argued.

The truth was, it was pretty hard to tell what the hell was going on with the signs posted above the parking space: "Alternate Street Parking Tue&Fri," "Meters Not In Effect Above Times," "No Parking 2AM-5AM," "6PM-midnight M-F metered parking," and a few others thrown in for good measure.

Noah stood by his interpretation. "We followed the rules. Monday through Friday, metered parking."

"Yeah, only it's Saturday now," Dylan corrected.

"Oops."

"Nice going, genius," Dylan shot back. "You said we could park here!"

It was true that Noah had said he could park there. Though Dylan was the unofficial leader of the group—based on his general confidence in life and his success with women—Noah was the brains of the operation. You don't get into Brown with Bs, and while Walker was smart (at least book smart), Noah was practically a genius. Dylan relied on that fact, and part of being a good leader was recognizing and utilizing other people's talents. So if Noah said, "You can park there," Dylan parked there without a second thought.

"All right, look, I'm sorry," Noah apologized. "But let's just forget the Cube for now and take a taxi to the party."

"Yeah, great idea, except the wristbands are in the car."

Noah was desperate, grasping at straws. "Maybe we can get new tickets somehow—"

Dylan would have liked to have been the one freaking out here—after all, it was his car that got towed to God knows where—but Noah had called dibs on being upset, so it was Dylan's job to make him feel better. Dylan put his arm around Noah's neck in a manly hug and cut to the chase. "This is a good thing, Noah. Sarah is moving on. It's only going to get easier from here on out."

Noah looked down. "I don't want it to get easier."

"Look. We're still going to the party. But we need the wristbands and that means we need the car. Okay?"

Noah was still stewing.

"Okay?" Dylan repeated.

"Yeah, okay."

"Come on," Dylan said as they started down the street. "Let's find out where the fuckers towed it to."

Onstage at der Freiheitsgestalt, the Chinese person was now completely bald and the naked haircutter took a bow. Everyone snapped and Walker half-heartedly joined them. He checked his watch. *How do I always wind up in these situations?*, he wondered.

Outside in the alley, Pike passed a joint to Haley. She took a deep drag.

Haley was in grad school in women's studies at N.Y.U. Normally she wouldn't have hung out with a high school kid like Pike, but he was funny, good-looking (in a young Sean Penn kind of way), and most importantly, he lived in the moment. Besides, grad school had opened her mind to the rich diversity of human existence and she was trying not to discriminate against upper-middle-class white people like herself.

On top of all that, Pike was a good listener and seemed to really understand where she was coming from. They were talking about some pretty deep shit and Haley was getting excited. "What I'm saying is," Haley continued, "we really need to explore the unstable nexus of gender, sexuality, race, and class in order to subvert the phallocentric hegemony."

"Oh, my God," Pike exclaimed with absolutely no idea what she was talking about, "I was just saying that same thing the other day!"

As Haley passed the joint back to Pike, it occurred to her that she was really starting to like this kid.

Back inside the club, a guy with piercings all over his body (like Hellraiser) exited the stage amid a chorus of snap applause. Thoroughly annoyed, Walker checked his watch again. He couldn't believe Pike had ditched him, and for all he knew, he wasn't coming back. He figured he'd give him ten more minutes before he bailed and tried to find Dylan and Noah.

Onstage, a goateed host dressed in a black turtleneck (*What a cliché*, Walker thought) introduced the next performer. "'A Decomposition,' by Genevieve," he announced dramatically. He stepped away, there was some snapping, and Genevieve took the stage.

Walker squinted to see her face but he was pretty sure it was *the weird girl from their school.*

She wasn't dressed in her usual flannel Nirvana-is-still-cool attire, and her hair and make-up were totally different. She actually looked... pretty.

She took the stage and sat on a stool. "Your essence destroys paper," she began.

> *This is what I learned,*
> *cleaning up the wine you spilled.*
> *On the table's dark lustrous skin.*

The audience seemed bored. This was after all pretty tame compared to the crazy shit that went before her.

But Walker was enraptured.

"Like opals, like your eyes," she continued. She was reciting it from memory and Walker could tell there was some truth and pain behind the poem.

> *The varnish holds a thousand colors captive.*
> *In its depths: the surface is black, but underneath,*

there stirs a lake of amethyst. While, still further down,

the uncrackable hardness of blood awaits.

As far as poetry was concerned, Walker thought this was pretty damn good. But the crowd disagreed and some murmurs began to rise from the dark room. Walker looked concerned for her. Apparently, she was bombing and from the look on her face, she knew it.

Still, she soldiered on.

I let the muscular tide pull my eyes swiftly downward,

a force that shatters the body and turns the mind to mist,

a mystifying force that drags me down

into the rainbow heart of the wood.

A woman from the crowd yelled out, "Do something!"

This rattled Genevieve. She seemed to lose her train of thought for a second but quickly recovered.

Which is more than a table,

a secret we tapped last night—

A man with a bull-like nose ring heckled, "You suck!"

Genevieve really flinched this time. The crowd was just not into this fairly pedestrian poem, and some people in the back got up to go have a smoke outside. Others just started talking among themselves. Walker couldn't believe how rude they were being. Onstage, Genevieve fought back tears.

"Last night," she repeated, "when we discovered a table can be a bird—"

The second heckler booed her.

Walker impulsively jumped up and turned to the guy behind him. "Shut the fuck up! She's a million times better than the freak with the pierced dick!"

Walker received some snaps from the audience members who agreed with him. He sat back down and Genevieve finished.

Like crushed fur: this wine I am now trying to soak up

with a paper towel. The napkin comes apart

in my trembling hand, it turns into a foam.

Genevieve bowed slightly to indicate it was over.

Walker stood and applauded. Like a normal person. With his hands. But Genevieve still hurried off the stage.

Over by the bar, she was met by Jerome, a pretentious-looking dude with hipster glasses and a vintage Army jacket. He was clearly older than her, maybe in his late-twenties, but when he hugged her, it was clear they were more than friends.

Walker got up and headed over to her. But when he arrived, for some reason Genevieve avoided eye contact with him.

"Hey. You go to my school, don't you?" Walker asked, just to be sure.

"Uh, yeah," Genevieve replied, grabbing Jerome's hand and clearly sending Walker a buzz-off vibe.

But Walker wasn't much for reading body language and continued, "You were great."

"Yeah, thanks. Good seeing you."

She turned her back to Walker but Jerome interjected, "Who's your friend?"

"Nobody—" she tried to say, but Walker offered, "I'm Walker. We go to high school together."

Genevieve buried her head in her hands and Walker slowly began to piece together that this was one of his frequent "oops" moments.

Jerome dropped Genevieve's hand and asked accusingly, "You're in high school?"

"Maybe," Genevieve replied with a sense of humor.

But Jerome was not to be trifled with. "You told me you were a post-doc candidate!"

"Relax. I'm eighteen," she reassured him.

But Jerome just took her gently by the face and imparted, "A relationship cannot survive if it is based on lies. One day you'll understand."

Then he kissed her forehead patronizingly and took off.

Genevieve watched him go then turned to Walker. "Great. Thanks a lot."

"Sorry." Walker did feel a little bad, but seriously, how was he supposed to know?

"Tonight is going *so* well," Genevieve sighed.

"I really did think you were great," Walker offered honestly.

Genevieve looked up with a tiny hint of a smile. "Really?"

"Really," Walker confirmed and met her smile with one of his own.

CHAPTER SIXTEEN

WALKER SAT AND had a beer with Genevieve. It turned out that not only did she make her own clothes, as she was known for around school, but she was something of a regular on the New York hipster scene. She regularly performed her poetry at clubs all over lower Manhattan and enjoyed going to art openings and hearing obscure indie bands play in unmarked venues.

Basically, Genevieve was an adult trapped in a high school girl's body. Her parents were professors, long divorced, her dad in English Literature at Columbia and her mom in Religious Studies at Trinity in Hartford. Genevieve lived with her mom, obviously, but went into the city whenever she wanted and just crashed at her dad's. He usually didn't even need to know she was coming. She had a key and there were many occasions when he was off at some conference anyway.

Genevieve didn't hate high school, she was just largely indifferent, biding her time till she went off to college. She never really fit in—she was just so far beyond the kids at Hall High, emotionally, intellectually, sexually, that she often felt like a detached investigative reporter on an undercover assignment as a high school student. She put up with the mentally unchallenging teachers—after all, they tried their best (except once when she came down hard on her health teacher who refused to accept her definition of "steroid" as "a terpenoid lipid with a sterane core and a hydrocarbon functional group")—and she put up with the juvenile antics of her classmates the best she could. Then she headed out to the city most Fridays to live her real life.

She had met Jerome at a wine tasting. He was a struggling writer working on a screenplay about a post-apocalyptic America where all meat has become poison to humans. (His day job was as a copyrighter for a pharmaceutical company.) Genevieve had long-ago made up the cover story of being a post-doc candidate, as she found that, despite what the popular porn genre would have you believe, older guys in fact found dating high school girls to be generally off-putting. They'd only been together less than a month, so it was no big loss to see him go. Still, her plans for the evening were ruined and now, oddly, she found herself tossing back a Guinness with one of her high school classmates.

"Do you come into the city a lot?" Walker asked innocently.

"Yeah. I usually read my poetry at 'The Pillow Room,' but I thought I'd give this place a try. Big mistake." She laughed.

"I think they're into stuff that's a little more... edgy," Walker offered by way of explanation. Onstage, a man in an ape suit was standing in front of a full-length mirror with a video camera, apparently recording the camera's reflection.

"Yeah," Genevieve agreed. "Maybe next time I'll get a midget to drag me around by my nipple rings."

Walker laughed. Then he felt the need for clarification and asked,

"You don't really have nipple rings, do you?"

Genevieve laughed and shook her head no.

Suddenly, Pike returned. He was alone, but thoroughly stoned. He saw Genevieve and thought he recognized her. "Hey, aren't you the girl from our school who makes her own clothes?"

Genevieve just smiled and replied, "Hi. Genevieve." She offered a hand and Pike shook it. Pike grabbed a chair from a nearby table and sat down with them.

"Where's Haley?" Walker asked.

"Taking the Browns to the Superbowl," Pike replied colorfully.

Walker rolled his eyes at Pike then turned back to Genevieve. "So where are you going next year?"

"Harvard," Genevieve replied matter-of-factly.

"Seriously?" Walker was thoroughly impressed.

Genevieve smiled. "Yeah. Why? Are you surprised?"

"Yeah," Walker admitted, before backtracking, "I mean, not that you're going there. You seem really smart. It's just... how did we never cross paths before?"

Genevieve leaned in and looked Walker in the eye. "We have A.P. Calculus together..." she felt insulted to have to remind him.

"I'm sorry. That's right," Walker said before quickly moving on to, "Well, I'm going to be in Boston, too. Just outside. Brandeis." Then he uttered his trademark line, "We should exchange emails."

Genevieve just stared at Walker for a second, then laughed in his face. Not in a terribly insulting way, just an honest reaction to what she correctly perceived as an incredibly dorky pick-up line.

She turned to Pike. "What about you, Pike? Where are you going next year?"

Pike smiled broadly, the same smug way he always did when he envisioned his future as a professional suntan-lotion applier. "University of the Pacific. Nothing but sand and surf."

But Genevieve looked confused. "University of the Pacific in California?"

"Is there another one?" Pike gloated. "Gonna major in bikini inspecting."

Genevieve raised an eyebrow. "You know that it's not actually on the ocean, right?"

"Yes, it is," Pike corrected her. "They have classes on surfing and a graduate lifeguard school."

"May be," Genevieve conceded, "but the University of the Pacific is in Stockton, near Sacramento. That's *northern* California. About two hours from the water."

Walker was really starting to enjoy this.

Pike shook his head. "No. That's not right."

"Yeah, it is," Genevieve said with certainty. "My cousin went there."

Pike looked crestfallen.

Genevieve was amazed at this oversight and asked, "Didn't you visit the school?"

"No," Pike admitted, "but in the catalog…"

Pike never finished that sentence. Instead, he just slumped down into his chair and muttered, "Fuck."

Genevieve put a sympathetic hand on Pike's shoulder. "You poor dumb bastard."

She smiled at Pike, and in that instant, Walker knew he was in love.

Walker uncharacteristically manned up, asking, "Hey, listen, do you want to go to a party with us?"

"Sure," Genevieve accepted the offer casually, adding the caveat, "as long as there's no dramatic haircutting involved."

"Hey, no promises," Walker joked.

They laughed.

Pike unfortunately was still a bit shell-shocked. His funk was turning into a full-blown depression when suddenly Haley returned, wrapping her arms around Pike in a romantic embrace.

"God, pot makes me so horny," she whispered in Pike's ear, but loudly enough for everyone to hear. "Want to go back to my place?"

Walker raised an eyebrow to Genevieve.

Pike emerged from his funk. "Yes, yes I do."

"Oh, and my roommate may want to join in," Haley added. "Is that a problem?"

"No, no it is not," Pike assured her.

Haley took Pike by the hand.

Pike was back!

Walker called after him, "Hey, what about the party?"

Pike shouted back, "I'll just meet you guys there." And he headed out with Haley.

On the way out the door, Pike asked Haley, "Your roommate's not a dude, is he?"

"No."

"Is she a fattie?"

"Uh, no."

"Does she have two legs?"

Haley stopped him. "Do you want to do this or not?"

"Yes, yes I do."

They continued out the door.

CHAPTER SEVENTEEN

DYLAN AND NOAH finally arrived at the towing company lot in Queens. They had to take a taxi because the subway seemed a little too complicated (and possibly dangerous at this time of night). The lot was located on Flatbush Boulevard, not the worst section of Queens but pretty close to it. Homeless people milled around on the corner and Noah was pretty sure he saw a prostitute giving a guy a blow job in an alley.

"Three Brothers Towing" was about what you might expect from a tow lot: a bunch of cars surrounded by a barbed wire fence. Random used car parts also littered some sections of the lot, and at the only apparent entrance was a small booth with a little plexiglass window. Behind the window was a fat, balding, greasy, douche-bag with "Anthony" emblazoned on his Three Brothers t-shirt. He was chewing tobacco and watching the Mets game recap on a little TV. The guys walked up to him.

"Hey, what's up, man?" Noah started.

"License plate" was all Anthony said. He didn't even look up.

Dylan answered, "933 TOX. Connecticut plates."

The guy punched it into his computer and read off from the computer screen, "One fifty city fine, eighty-eight towing charge, nineteen impound fee, mileage is thirty-eight fifty. Total is... two ninety-five fifty."

Dylan looked at Noah expectantly. After all, it was Noah who got him towed.

Noah rolled his eyes but didn't put up a fight. He pulled out his emergency credit card and passed it through the little window.

But the guy slid it back. "No credit cards, dipshit." He pointed to a sign above Noah's head that read, "Cash only."

Noah checked his wallet and turned back to Dylan. "I don't have that much cash."

Dylan checked his. "I've only got forty bucks left."

Anthony didn't look up from the TV as he said, "ATM across the street."

Noah saw the ATM outside a bodega and the two of them crossed the street. As Noah began the process of withdrawing his cash, he commented, "Is tonight everything you dreamed it would be?"

But Dylan was still a true believer, replying, "Don't be so negative. You're going to remember this shit forever."

"I'm gonna remember this three hundred dollars, that's for sure."

"You got me towed, Ivy League, you pay the piper," Dylan said with a little chuckle.

Just then, a voice boomed behind them: "Yo! Gimme your wallet!"

Startled, Noah turned and saw a gang of scary Albanian dudes. Noah had no idea if they were really Albanians—they could have been from any Eastern European country as far as he knew—but he had read an article about the Albanian mob recently and the idea had stuck with him.

Noah tried to reason with them. "No, wait, I need this to get our car—"

But the lead guy just pushed Noah to the ground and grabbed his wallet.

Dylan thought seriously about making a stand but it was six against two, and who knew what these guys were packing.

The gang leader turned to Dylan and ordered, "You too, Zac Efron!"

Dylan reluctantly handed over his wallet.

The transaction complete, the gang turned to leave when...

A melodic version of "Short Skirt/Long Jacket" started emanating from Dylan's pants.

Dylan tried to act nonchalant, ignoring his ringing phone, but the guy with his wallet just smiled, like, *Nice try.*

"Phones," he ordered.

Now Dylan tried to bargain. "Come on, man. I just got this."

The guy punched Dylan in the stomach and took his phone. Noah handed over his own phone voluntarily and the gang took off.

Walker and Genevieve stood in front of the empty space where the Cube was once parked, Walker on Genevieve's phone. "No answer," Walker reported.

Walker hung up and gave Genevieve her phone back.

Noah was pretty shaken by the mugging. "Are you all right?" he asked as he helped Dylan up.

"Yeah, great," Dylan joked, still doubled over in pain.

"We need to call the police!"

"Yeah, I'm sure they'll put out an APB," Dylan mocked.

But Noah was pretty worked up and ran back across the street to the tow lot. At the booth, he reported to Anthony, "We just got robbed!"

"Yeah, I saw that," Anthony replied with not even faux concern.

Noah was incensed. "You saw it?! Why didn't you do something?! Call the police!"

Anthony finally looked up. "Ooh, or maybe Batman!"

Dylan just stood there, unsurprised by the reaction Noah was getting.

But Noah was still trying to reason with the guy. "Look, we're from out of town, obviously. I'm just trying to meet up with my girlfriend at this party on Front Street. If you'd just give us our car back so we can get out of here, I will send you a check, I promise."

"Yeah, that's not gonna happen."

"This is fucking ridiculous! They took our money and our phones. What are we supposed to do now?"

Anthony just shrugged.

Noah was desperate. He started racking his brains for a solution. Then an idea floated into his brain that was so perfect that Noah impressed even himself.

"Okay, how about this? If you give us our car back now, we'll pay you in weed."

For the first time in their brief relationship, Anthony was finally paying attention to Noah. "Excuse me?"

Dylan pulled Noah aside. "Are you crazy?"

But Noah was confident. "Do you want to get out of here or not?"

He returned to the window. "There's a brick of weed in the car. You can have an ounce in exchange for giving us our car back."

Anthony thought about it for a second. "What's the plate number again?"

Dylan reminded him, "933 TOX."

Anthony punched up the number again and got the location of the car. Dylan passed the key to him through the window and Anthony instructed, "Hang on."

Anthony walked across the lot and found the car. He used Dylan's key to unlock it and looked around in the back seat. There was Pike's book bag. Anthony opened it and saw the brick of marijuana. He looked around, then took the whole book bag.

But when he returned to the window, all he said was, "Sorry, I couldn't find any weed in your car." And with that, he passed the key back to Dylan through the window.

Noah was confused. "What? Yes, there is. There was a book bag—"

Anthony interrupted him with a new, menacing tone of voice, "I said there wasn't any weed in your car." Then he turned around and started to walk away, revealing Pike's book bag on his shoulder.

Noah went ballistic. He started rattling the chain link fence. "You fucking asshole! Give us back our weed! This guy stole our weed!"

Dylan grabbed Noah and tried to get him to calm down.

Anthony returned to the fence and threatened, "Get out of here, you bridge and tunnel pricks, before I really do call the cops!"

Noah spat at him and yelled, "Fuck you!" but the guy just gave Noah the finger and walked away. Noah rattled the fence some more, spewing bile before Dylan was finally able to pull him away.

Noah glared at Dylan accusingly. "Are you happy?"

"What? This is my fault somehow? You're the one who said we could park there."

"I wanted to go straight to the party!" Noah reminded him.

"Who cares about the fucking party?!" Dylan was sick of Noah's bullshit. "So you saw Sarah with some guy. Who cares! Can't you just hang out with your friends for once in your life?!"

Then, something occurred to Noah and he actually smiled. "Oh, my God. You're jealous."

"Yeah, right," Dylan scoffed. "Sarah is not that hot."

"Not of me, dumbass. You're jealous of Sarah."

Dylan laughed derisively.

But Noah was sure he was onto something here. "You are. You want me all to yourself."

"You are so gay."

Noah continued on, like a detective about to break a suspect. "No, it's true. That's what this is all about. You don't like sharing me with her."

Dylan got in Noah's face. "Well, what's so wrong about wanting to spend some time with my best friend—"

"Because you made me break up with her!" Noah screamed in his face.

Dylan escalated things, taking a step closer. "*You* came to *me* and asked what to do! I was just being a good friend."

"No, you were being a selfish asshole, like always!"

Dylan exploded: "What does it matter?! You and Sarah are *over*! And whether it's now or two months from now, you better get used to the idea of her sucking other guys' cocks!"

Noah *punched Dylan in the face!*

Dylan came back and tackled Noah, knocking them both to the ground. They rolled around, punching and wrestling until Noah finally broke free. The two of them stood up, panting.

"Fuck you!" Noah yelled.

"No, fuck you!" Dylan shot back.

Dylan spat blood onto the street. "Don't you get it?! This—" he said, gesturing all around him, "This is over!"

Noah didn't know what he was talking about.

"Everything is over! Your life as you know it is *gone*! Your friends. Your family. This chapter has come to an end. And spoiler alert, we're not going to be best friends in chapter two."

Noah just glared at him for a moment before saying, "You're a real fucking dick."

And with that, Noah started to walk away.

Dylan suddenly realized he had gone too far and called out, "Noah, wait. Stop. Noah!"

CHAPTER EIGHTEEN

BACK ON CANAL Street, Haley escorted a still very stoned Pike into her dark apartment. She closed the door behind them and the two were immediately all over each other, kissing sloppy kisses and feeling each other up. Pike didn't believe in following the traditional path around the bases, and quickly reached down into her jeans.

Then, from out of the kitchen came Cassandra, a gorgeous redhead even hotter than Haley. Pike couldn't believe it. He figured on the taxi ride over that maybe she would be a six, or a seven at best. After all, girls either intentionally overrated their friends' looks or simply had no idea. But Cassandra was tall and skinny like a model and her long, straight hair fell down to the middle of her back. She was in her twenties, like Haley, and she watched Pike and Haley getting busy for a moment before commenting, "That is so hot."

Haley came up for air. "Look what I brought home for us," she purred to Cassandra.

"Nice," Cassandra replied seductively. Then she came over and started massaging Pike's chest.

Pike was a little nervous. "Uh, hi. Jeff Pike. People call me Pike."

"I hope that's truth in advertising," Cassandra whispered before grabbing his crotch.

Pike looked around. "Is this a porno? Am I being recorded for some voyeur video?"

The girls just laughed and started kissing each other.

Pike didn't need an engraved invitation. He joined in.

Luckily for Walker, Genevieve knew exactly where Front Street was. With few options presenting themselves, they decided to go to the party in the hopes that the other guys had found their way there, too.

Front Street was near the South Street Seaport and housed some fish processing factories, a few trendy lofts, and a lot of abandoned buildings. It was an area of Manhattan where few people spent any real time, unless they were executive chefs at a seafood restaurant.

The party itself was off Front Street on an unnamed alley. A long line of people stretched down the block.

Near the end of the line, Walker tried once again to reach Dylan and Noah with Genevieve's phone. "Still no answer," he reported and handed the phone back to her.

Genevieve looked tired. "Well, it's getting late anyway. I should catch the train back..."

"No, wait," Walker pleaded. "It's early. We're already here."

"How are we supposed to get in?"

She had a point. The hologram-etched wristbands were in the Cube and this wasn't the kind of party that sold tickets at the door.

Walker's growing infatuation with Genevieve forced his brain into overdrive. He wanted this to work out more than anything. Something inside of him was telling him this was an important moment that could change his life and he couldn't just let it slip away. He needed a way into that party.

Then, proving that necessity truly is the mother of invention, a thought materialized from the ether and Walker announced confidently, "I've got an idea."

A few minutes later, Walker and Genevieve walked around back to the loading dock, carrying an empty Styrofoam cooler they had found in a pile of trash in an empty lot. The loading dock was busy with dozens of people hauling more booze and equipment into the party. Walker and Genevieve held either side of the cooler, pretending it had some weight to it. At the entrance was a party coordinator, basically an overweight guy in his thirties wearing a Nine Inch Nails concert t-shirt and carrying a clipboard. He was checking off each person that entered, and double-checked everything against his inventory list. He was the sole gatekeeper to the back entrance.

As the two approached him, he questioned, "What's this supposed to be?"

"Dry ice," Walker answered a little too quickly.

The guy checked his clipboard. "You're not on the list."

"Yeah, we are," Walker replied, trying his best to sound convincing. "Check it again."

But instead, the coordinator looked them up and down and noticed something was missing. "I'm sorry, where's your event badge?"

Amazingly, Walker played it cool, taking an aggressive stance. "Hello? We're not event staff. We're with Smirnoff Ice, one of your premium beverage vendors? And you've got about ten seconds before this dry ice sublimates. You want to be responsible if that happens?"

Genevieve was impressed, but kept a straight face. The party coordinator looked Walker over and Walker was sure the guy had bought it.

Instead, he said, "Do I look like an idiot? What are you, nineteen?" The guy lifted the top off the cooler and rolled his eyes at the lack of dry ice, or anything else, inside.

Walker looked embarrassed and put down the empty Styrofoam cooler. He sighed, defeated.

But then Genevieve stepped up and took a crack at it. "Okay, fine, you got us," she admitted, "but can you at least do me a favor?"

The guy looked at her skeptically and said, "Yeah, what's that?"

"Look over there," she requested, nodding to the left.

Confused, the guy instinctively looked over, and in a flash, Genevieve started running! She easily made it past the guy and into the building before he had time to react. Unfortunately, Walker was also taken by surprise, and by the time his brain told his feet to follow Genevieve, the guy was crouched in a defensive posture, guarding the entrance like an American Gladiator.

Walker crouched as well, his eyes darting left and right, looking for a way in. Finally, Walker locked eyes with the man. Maybe there was no way this guy was letting Walker get by, but there was also no way Walker was letting Genevieve go off without him. Walker studied the situation, and his years of education and experience told him there was only one solution. Walker kicked him in the balls.

"I'm sorry," Walker said as the guy crumpled to the ground, and he honestly was.

Walker ran.

Walker found Genevieve inside the loading dock. They stopped to catch their breath and saw no one was after them.

"What happened? I thought I lost you."

"How about a little head's up next time?" Walker complained, his adrenaline still pumping.

"Sorry, my senses are finely attuned to seek out weaknesses in my opponents."

"Huh?"

"I spent the first nine years of my life training in a Shaolin temple," Genevieve explained with a straight face.

"Seriously?"

"No, dumbass."

This is the coolest girl I have ever met in my life, Walker thought.

Genevieve smiled and pulled Walker down the hallway toward the party.

The music grew louder and they could feel the electricity in the air as they snaked down the back hallway toward the party. But when they turned the corner and actually laid eyes on it, it was too much for even Genevieve's brain to process all at once. There were simply too many things going on. The size and scope of the party were overwhelming.

There were easily more than a thousand people partying. A celebrity DJ manned a massive sound system usually reserved for Metallica concerts. Actual go-go dancers in steel birdcages were spaced around the dance floor. A well-dressed model with a Capuchin monkey on her shoulder walked by. People were drinking, dancing, making out, and having the time of their lives. It was like an indoor Woodstock crossed with a modern rave.

"Jesus," was all Walker could say.

"Check that out," Genevieve said, nodding to the right. Some hot girls were running and jumping face-first onto a Slip & Slide (creating nice wet t-shirts in the process).

"Isn't that iCarly?" Genevieve asked, amazed.

"Look at the bar," Walker gasped. It was half a block long with about thirty bartenders.

"I think that girl is naked," Genevieve pointed out. Sure enough, a circulating Cuervo Girl's top was painted-on to look like Pancho Villa.

She saw the two of them gaping and stopped to ask, "Shot of Cuervo?"

"I'll do one," Genevieve volunteered.

"Sure, me too," Walker joined in.

The girl had no shotglasses, only liters of Cuervo strapped to her waist. She pulled out both bottles like a gunslinger and poured a shot directly into each of their mouths.

"José Cuervo," she seemed required to say, "proud sponsor of Stark Raving Mad 2012." And then she took off in search of another customer.

Walker and Genevieve looked at each other for a moment and smiles crept across their faces. This was going to be fun.

In Haley's bedroom—or was it Cassandra's?—Pike was in his underwear kissing and dry humping the two naked girls. This was the hottest thing he'd ever imagined, let alone actually done, and Cassandra grabbed his crotch again.

But instead of her sexy voice, Cassandra seemed disappointed. "What's the matter?" she teased. "Not sexy enough for you?"

Pike had no idea what she was talking about. He was too caught up in the kissing and groping to notice that he was apparently trying to shoot pool with a rope. He had Whiskey Dick… E.D.… Flaccid Phallus… That's right. Pike was limp.

He turned bright red.

"This has never happened before," Pike blurted out. And it hadn't.

"Don't worry about it," Haley reassured him. "Probably just the weed."

But Pike was starting to panic. "No, I can do this!" he announced as he furiously started beating the bishop.

All the action came to a screeching halt as the girls sat up and watched Pike trying to get himself hard. And he was not being gentle.

"Jesus, you're going to pull it off!" Haley warned.

"Here," Cassandra cooed, the voice of reason, "Let us help."

They tried, each individually and together, both orally and manually, but after a painfully un-arousing half-hour, the girls gave up and just sat up in bed, frustrated.

But Pike was not going to let this beat him. He was going to die trying. He attempted to reassure the dubious girls, "Look, I can do this. Trust me, I am the master of my own domain. Just don't go anywhere."

He excused himself and headed into the bathroom. Pike stared at himself in the mirror, standing there naked, and took a deep breath. His brain was still foggy from the pot, so he splashed some water on his face and tried to clear his head. He jumped up and down a couple times, trying to psych himself up, then reached down and started masturbating once again.

He ran through a slate of mental images: Selena Gomez. Catholic schoolgirls. That yogurt commercial. Walker's mom.

He looked down. Nothing.

Then he spoke out loud, "Come on, buddy. Don't let me down. You do this for me, I swear to God I will never smoke pot again!"

In that moment he realized something. He looked off into the distance and cursed, "Shut up, Dylan."

CHAPTER NINETEEN

DYLAN AND NOAH sat on the curb ten feet apart, not speaking to each other. Noah had sensibly abandoned his attempt at walking home or hitchhiking, but after their fight there wasn't much left to say.

Dylan broke the silence. "You remember your first day of kindergarten?"

Noah looked over at him. He wasn't sure if he was ready yet to start talking to Dylan again or, even if he were ready, if this was some sort of rhetorical question. He decided to respond and said, "No."

"Me either," Dylan replied, starting to get into one of his nostalgic moods. "But I remember we used to take naps on these ratty carpets. I used to hate taking those naps." He thought about it for a second then added, "I love naps now."

Noah was getting annoyed. For a straight shooter, Dylan could be pretty cryptic at times, and he was the worst when he was trying to be philosophical. "What's your point?" Noah demanded.

Dylan explained, "I only remember bits and pieces. High school is so real compared to back then. It's like... sometimes I feel like my life is something that's happening to someone else and I'm just watching."

Noah studied him and decided this was Dylan opening up. Noah let down his wall a bit and replied, "Yeah."

"Ten years from now high school is going to be like kindergarten. Our brains are just going to file it under shit that happened a long time ago."

Dylan was actually making sense and Noah thought about what he said.

Dylan looked at Noah and caught his eye before admitting, "I'm not going to UConn next year."

"What do you mean?"

"I'm going into the Army. I enlisted." Dylan had been thinking about how to tell his friends for months now but had never really come up with any clever scenarios, so this seemed as good a time as any.

"What? No, you didn't." Noah was taken aback. It seemed like a joke, but Dylan didn't look like he was joking.

"Yeah, I did," Dylan said matter-of-factly. "I go to basic training next Saturday."

"Are you being serious?" Noah asked in a shaky voice. But Noah could see that Dylan *was* being serious. Suddenly, Noah exploded. "What the fuck, Dylan?! Are you crazy?!"

Noah stood up, actually mad at Dylan.

Dylan stood as well and walked toward Noah. He shook his head, "I knew you wouldn't understand."

"Yeah, you're right I don't understand. We're still at war, asshole!"

"You know what? Forget it. I'm sorry I told you."

Noah was stunned. He didn't know what to say. Then the pieces just fell together in his mind. "So that's what this whole trip is all about. This *is* your last weekend with us."

Dylan looked him in the eye with a little guilty nod and admitted, "Yeah."

But Noah was still trying to wrap his head around this. "Why, Dylan? At least try to explain it to me."

Dylan took a deep breath and tried to make it make sense. "Look. Everything's always been easy for me. Okay, maybe I don't get straight As, but I feel like I've always had things pretty well figured out."

Noah listened.

"I need this challenge. I'm going to try to make Army Rangers."

"This isn't a video game."

"Yeah, I know," Dylan said somberly.

Noah could see this was not a spur-of-the-moment thing for Dylan. This was a decision he'd probably agonized over, and he'd done it alone. "What'd your Dad say?"

"He's pretty pissed," Dylan admitted.

They laughed. But Noah was still speechless. He just shook his head.

This was one of those life-altering moments you remember forever, and the fact that Noah could step out of the moment and see it happening was surreal. It was all too much for Noah to process. He closed his eyes and tried to block it all out.

But then a thought flashed into Noah's brain. This moment, right now, was when things would change. It would all be different from here on out.

Dylan was right. This chapter of their lives *was* over, and no matter how hard they tried, their relationship was going to be different now. They had been taking each other for granted all these years, blindly marching toward the precipice of graduation as if nothing would change when they fell into the abyss. But now he realized that they would never be this close again. Never spend another weekend together like this. Sure, they'd email and text and maybe see each other over the summer. But the fundamental nature of their bond was breaking. Forever.

He looked over at Dylan and suddenly felt a surge of emotion. Dylan was right next to him, here and now. He could reach out and touch him. This moment felt so real. But it also felt like it was slipping away. A distance was forming between them and even now he could see it starting. A drifting apart. They were growing up, Noah guessed, and it felt like shit.

Dylan saw it in Noah's eyes and gave him a reassuring smile, one he'd given Noah a thousand times before, one that said, *Don't worry. It'll all be okay.*

Noah nodded.

Then Dylan changed the subject, turning back to Noah apologetically. "If you love Sarah so much, why'd you listen to me?"

"Because I always listen to you," Noah admitted. And there was the problem. Noah knew it and Dylan knew it. With great power comes great responsibility.

"I know. I'm sorry. The truth is I don't have all the answers."

This was a rare admission for Dylan, and Noah appreciated that he'd said it. Suddenly, Noah thought of something.

"Come on. I've got an idea."

"What is it?"

"We get the car, then we go to the party and rescue my girlfriend." Noah was re-energized.

Dylan forced a smile. "Sounds like a plan."

As they turned to leave, Noah caught Dylan's gaze. Dylan was tearing up.

Noah had never seen Dylan like this before. Something in his eye. Was he afraid? Noah stopped and gave Dylan a big hug.

And Dylan didn't want to let go.

Finally, Noah pulled away and said, "Come on. Let's go."

And with that, Noah led them down the street.

CHAPTER TWENTY

WALKER AND GENEVIEVE were now dancing in the foam pit, as bubbles from an industrial-strength foam machine filled the floor. They were laughing, having a great time. The mash-up of MGMT's "Time to Pretend" and Talib Kweli's "Listen!!!" ended and Genevieve pulled Walker away from the pit for a breather.

Walker looked at Genevieve. "How is it possible that we've gone to the same school together for all these years and we've never spoken once until tonight, five days before graduation?"

"Can I be honest with you?"

"Of course."

"We have spoken before," she corrected. "A lot of times. You just don't remember. Because I guess for some reason you decided you already had enough friends."

Walker looked down, embarrassed. "I'm a fucking asshole."

"Yeah, pretty much."

He looked up into her eyes, a little sad. "You are so cool. I can't believe I missed... knowing you."

Genevieve laughed.

Walker leaned in and kissed her. No debate, hand-wringing, or inner turmoil. It just felt right, and for the first time in his life Walker lived in the moment.

After a long kiss, they came up for air and she looked him in the eye. Without saying a word, she took him by the hand and led him up some stairs in the back of the hall.

Noah and Dylan continued walking down Flatbush Avenue until they arrived at a crowded Greek diner with cars parked in the lot.

"There we go," Noah announced and headed inside.

Dylan had no idea what Noah was doing, but followed him anyway.

Inside the diner, Noah walked up to the empty hostess stand and shouted over the noise, "Who here parked in the handicapped space?!"

Everyone stopped eating and looked over at him, but no one answered. Dylan played along, still completely in the dark on this one.

A heavy manager in a burgundy dress shirt (but no tie) finally came over to them and asked, "Can I help you?"

"Someone parked illegally in the handicapped parking space."

"Sorry about that but what do you want me to do about it?"

Dylan wondered the same thing.

Noah got in the guy's face. "I want you to call the towing company and have them towed."

"Come on. Just park in some other space."

Noah raised his voice dramatically. "Yeah, and I guess my buddy in the car should have just parked in 'some other space' back in Kandahar when that IED blew his legs off!"

Checkmate.

The manager stared blankly at Noah and Dylan then turned and shouted out: "Who parked in the handicapped space?!"

Still, no one answered.

Noah stared at him expectantly.

"I'm sorry. I'll take care of it."

The manager picked up the phone and called the tow company. Satisfied, Noah and Dylan headed outside to wait.

The minute they were out of earshot, Dylan grabbed Noah's arm. "What the hell are you doing?"

But there was no time to explain just yet, and Noah simply replied, "Help me with this sign."

Noah went over to the blue handicapped parking sign attached to a cylindrical concrete block which stood, in fact, in front of an empty space. But Noah starting rolling it away from the empty space toward the adjacent spot where a Chevy Malibu was parked.

Dylan finally understood what Noah was doing and grabbed the sign to help roll it over to the other space. When they were done it looked like *that* car had parked in the handicapped space.

Dylan smiled. "Pretty sneaky, sis. Now what?"

Noah looked around, saw no one else in the parking lot, then elbowed the Malibu's rear tail light, breaking the glass.

"What are you doing?!"

"Relax," Noah assured him. "I saw this once on 'The Wire.'"

He cleared out the broken glass and plastic from the tail light cavity and stuck his hand into the hole. He fished around for a moment, looking for the emergency trunk release, when suddenly, voilà! The trunk popped open.

"Holy shit, that was awesome!" Dylan exclaimed, thoroughly impressed.

"Hop in," Noah said with a sly grin.

"Are you serious?"

"It's a Trojan Horse," Noah explained. He patted Dylan on the back and with a hint of condescension added, "Didn't you ever read the *Iliad*?"

Dylan answered in his best yokel voice, "Nuh uh, they only learned us 'See Spot Run' in remedial English."

Noah climbed in and Dylan followed. Then Noah closed the trunk down on them.

It was pretty damn dark inside the trunk. There were flares, a dirty spare tire, and some rags that looked like they were used to clean a rhino's ass. But the guys didn't care. Their hearts were pounding with excitement and this was one of the craziest things they'd ever done.

"Now what?" Dylan asked.

"Now we wait."

CHAPTER TWENTY-ONE

PIKE CAME OUT of the bathroom defeated. He'd tried everything, replayed in his mind every porn clip he'd ever seen, and rubbed his member raw. But nothing worked; the drugs in his system were just too much to overcome. So he came out of the bathroom with his head hung low.

Cassandra saw his sad puppy-dog eyes and asked, "You want me to shove this up your ass?" She held up a giant purple dildo.

"Is that a trick question?"

"To stimulate your prostate," Haley explained. "It'll help you get hard."

Pike looked at them. Sex with two beautiful girls and the only price was a monster dildo up the ass.

Pike pondered the decision for what seemed like an eternity.

He sighed. "Have fun, ladies."

And he sulked away.

Pike retrieved his clothes, got dressed, and let himself out. He walked out of the building, sullen. On the top step of the brownstone, Pike stopped and looked down at his crotch.

And gave it the finger.

"FUCK YOU!!!"

He wandered off.

Up on the roof of the abandoned fish processing plant, the city lights sparkled and the Brooklyn Bridge towered only a stone's throw away. Walker was on top of Genevieve, making out with her.

This was truly unlike anything Walker had ever done. He'd had girlfriends on occasion and had even made out with a few random girls at parties. But this was different. He really liked this girl, and thinking about her made his stomach hurt. Maybe this was love, Walker considered.

Whatever it was, it was nice. And more importantly, it was easy. Everything was easy with Genevieve. They just clicked, and Walker didn't find himself second-guessing everything he did. She had led him upstairs and Walker smoothly initiated the romance without any planning whatsoever.

Things were moving slowly forward. Walker had her topless and was letting his hands roam all over her body. It was getting pretty hot and Genevieve was giving Walker the green light to keep going.

As much as Walker wanted to stay in the moment, something deep inside of him pulled him out and he had a moment of self-reflection. *This is it*, he thought. *I'm really going to do it.* He'd built up this moment in his mind so much over his entire adolescence that there was simply no way to let it happen without at least a little out-of-body sense of awe.

But this stoked the fires in Walker's brain, and once those neurons were firing, it was hard to turn them off. A thought leapt into his head where it was weighed, analyzed, and approved for speaking.

Walker stopped kissing Genevieve and started to confess, "I should tell you, I've never done this before. So I might not be that good. I mean, I don't really know—"

But before he could get the whole speech out, she covered his mouth with her hand.

"Don't talk."

She removed her hand.

"Okay," Walker agreed.

"What did I just say?"

"Don't talk."

"And are you following my instructions?"

"No."

"Still talking..."

Walker finally just smiled. He kissed her and they started to make love.

Back in the trunk, Noah and Dylan passed the time talking. It was obviously an odd place to bond, but after they got used to the smell and overcame their claustrophobia, it was kind of nice.

They talked about the Army and what Dylan would have to do to make Rangers. They talked about memories, like Noah's tenth birthday party where Jack Unger laughed so hard a pepperoni came flying out of his nose. And they talked about Sarah, about how maybe all the fighting was really just them being scared for the future.

During a lull in the conversation, Dylan asked, "You know what a wingman is?"

"Yeah. I'm supposed to keep the ugly friend occupied while you bang the hottie."

"No, seriously. In air tactics."

Noah shrugged.

Dylan explained. "People think it's all about following the leader and doing what he says, but the wingman's real job is to *protect* the leader."

Noah looked at Dylan, his face illuminated by a sliver of light coming through the busted tail light. "What are you saying?"

Dylan met his eyes. "The wingman doesn't need the leader. The leader needs the wingman."

A tear welled in Noah's eye. It was the most emotional, heart-felt thing he'd ever heard Dylan say. And he was just about to return the sentiment when suddenly, they heard a noise.

Noah peeked out through the tail light. "It's them. Three Brothers Towing."

They heard some more noises like a chain, some metal scraping, and a hydraulic, then the car jerked up and Noah fell into Dylan. Dylan screamed as Noah's knee lodged into Dylan thigh, but Noah shushed him.

Some more noises, then the car started moving. As the car was towed away, the guys bumped their heads and got tossed around the trunk.

Dylan looked at Noah. "I hope you know what you're doing."

"Me, too," he replied.

A thought popped into Noah's head sometime during the bumpy

ten-minute ride to the impound lot. What if they were taking them to one of those car crushers? It made no sense—he knew they didn't crush cars for parking illegally—but what if there were a mix-up? Or the Three Brothers just did it anyway, as a goof? Would they ever even find their lifeless bodies, compacted into a tiny cube like Wiley E. Coyote in a Road Runner cartoon? And if they did, what would they say? All he needed was the headline "Gay Lovers Suicide Pact" haunting his parents for the rest of their lives.

He was just about to tell this to Dylan when suddenly the car stopped. It was lowered to the ground, they heard some more noises, then it was quiet.

The guys waited another minute to be sure, then Noah slowly pulled the emergency release and the trunk opened.

He peeked out. Sure enough, they were inside the towing lot.

Noah saw that the coast was clear and slowly climbed out. He silently helped Dylan out of the trunk, then motioned to him and pointed toward the back of the lot.

It was the Cube.

The two slinked across the lot until they arrived at the Cube. Dylan took his keys and manually unlocked the passenger door to avoid any noise. He did the same to the driver's door and got in. They closed their doors without a sound.

Once again, their hearts were pounding. Sure, it was Dylan's own car they were stealing, but it sure felt like grand theft auto to them.

Dylan put the key in the ignition and whispered, "You ready?"

"Let's do this."

Dylan turned the key.

Suddenly, Wreckx-N-Effect blasted from the radio, blaring "ALL I

WANNA DO IS ZOOMA-ZOOM-ZOOM-ZOOM IN A BOOM-BOOM!"

Dylan darted for the volume control and turned off the "Rump Shaker."

Noah's heart started beating again as they waited a moment to see if anyone heard them.

Sure enough, Anthony came out of his little booth to see where the noise had come from. And he was soon joined by his other two brothers, Sal and Vinnie, who came out of the main building.

"Shit," Dylan sighed.

But there was no turning back now.

"Punch it!" Noah ordered.

Dylan floored the accelerator and the Cube raced out of the lot. Unfortunately, the gate was locked.

As they zoomed forward, Dylan screamed, "What about the fence?!"

"Ram it!"

"*That's* your plan?!"

"I didn't think this far ahead!"

But the discussion was moot.

BOOM!

They rammed the fence.

One side of the gate exploded off its hinges and shot up into the air while the other side swung open. The Cube accelerated onto the main street and the gate landed behind the car.

Dylan looked back in the rear view mirror. Both of them were pumped up on adrenaline and couldn't believe it.

"Holy shit!" Noah exclaimed.

Back in the lot, the original asshole, Anthony, yelled, "They're stealing that car!"

Vinnie shouted, "Mother fuckers!"

"Get them!" Sal ordered.

The three brothers jumped into their cheesy muscle car and sped after them.

It was roughly two a.m., the Cube was racing along Flatbush Avenue at sixty miles per hour, and three insane Italians were chasing them in a Camaro.

Noah saw the Camaro gaining on them and yelled, "Head towards the bridge!"

"Which way?!"

"There!"

The Cube turned onto the Manhattan Bridge.

In the Camaro, Vinnie, the youngest of the three brothers, and sporting a thick bushy moustache not unlike Super Mario, yelled from the passenger seat, "They're taking the bridge!"

Sal, the eldest, with no official beard, just a thick layer of five o'clock shadow, floored it.

Still, the guys had a good thirty-second lead. The bridge dumped the Cube out onto Canal Street and as they sped along, they saw a guy walking.

"Pike?" Dylan wondered aloud, not sure if he was right.

Noah yelled, "Stop! Stop the car!"

Dylan slammed on the brakes and the Cube skidded toward the curb, leaving a trail of burnt rubber. The noise got Pike's attention and he looked up just as the Cube screeched to a halt right in front of him.

He leaned in through Noah's open window. "Hey, guys."

Noah screamed, "Get in!!!"

Pike saw that some shit was going down and quickly jumped into the back seat.

Dylan peeled out.

Stopping for Pike had given the Camaro time to catch up, and now the Italians were only a few yards behind them.

"Left! Head south!" Noah ordered.

Dylan swerved onto Lafayette Street.

Pike was fairly calm, given the circumstances, and asked simply, "Hey, what's going on?"

"It's a long story," Dylan replied as he ran a red light.

Noah looked out the back window and reported, "They're still after us!"

Dylan swerved again, this time making a left U-turn onto Dover Street.

The Cube passed the Camaro going the other way and Dylan quickly turned, hoping to lose them.

Pike looked around. "Hey! Where's my weed?"

Noah looked back at him. "Yeah, about that..."

Dylan quickly pulled up under the Brooklyn Bridge, stopped, and turned off the lights. He left the car idling, just in case, but for all intents and purposes, they were in silent running mode.

They waited.

You could almost hear their hearts pounding.

Then, Dylan saw the Camaro driving down the perpendicular Lafayette Street and whispered, "There!"

But the Camaro kept going.

They'd lost them.

All three of them breathed a sigh of relief.

They waited another moment in silence to be sure, then Dylan turned off the ignition. He turned back to Pike. "So, we've been hiding in trunks and stealing cars from the Insane Clown Posse. What have you been up to?"

"Nothing," Pike replied sadly. "Abso-fucking-lutely nothing."

Noah looked around. "Where are we?"

Then Dylan spotted something.

"Look."

The street sign. It read "Front Street."

The guys looked at each other, amazed. They were looking at the alley behind Front Street, the mysterious unnamed road that didn't appear on any Google map.

They broke out into big smiles, then Dylan grabbed the wristbands from the change holder and they got out of the car.

CHAPTER TWENTY-TWO

THE GUYS WALKED up the small street lined with boarded-up buildings, empty lots, and rubble. But as they got closer to the alley, they saw more and more people, and everyone was headed in the same direction.

Toward the party.

The three of them started to feel the excitement and energy from the crowd of young people waiting in line to get in. People were chatting in this festive atmosphere, and strangers became friends as the line moved along. When the guys finally reached the front of the line, they showed the bouncer their wristbands and entered the party.

As they stepped in and the deep bass of the thumping David Guetta tune "Sexy Bitch" vibrated their teeth, they were immediately in awe of the size and scope of this party. The sheer number of people and the size of the warehouse were unlike anything they'd ever seen before. After all, this was a party that companies *sponsored*. It had a *budget*. People planned and organized it and it took a *crew* to set up.

They just stood there, stunned.

Noah was the first to snap out of it. "I'm going to go try to find Sarah."

"Good luck, man," Dylan said, and he meant it.

Noah knew Dylan was rooting for him. He always was.

"Thanks."

And Noah headed out into the crowd.

Pike turned to Dylan. "Sarah's here?"

Dylan smiled. "It's a long story."

Pike and Dylan went over to the bar and in no time they were both enjoying a couple of cold Smirnoff Ices, proud sponsor of Stark Raving Mad 2012.

"So where's Walker?" Pike asked.

Dylan raised an eyebrow. "Wasn't he with you?"

"Nope, we split up at this freaky barber shop in Soho," Pike inaccurately summarized. "Last I saw him he was chatting up some girl." Then he added confidentially, "P.S., he didn't do it with that hot Latina chick."

Dylan sighed, "Poor Walker."

Walker and Genevieve got dressed. The sex had been nice. Walker didn't have comically premature ejaculation like in every teen comedy he'd ever seen. Maybe because he wasn't nervous like he thought he'd be. Or maybe, the thought crossed his mind, because he actually *was* good at it. Whatever the reason, it lasted long enough for him and maybe even long enough for Genevieve.

It was weird. He'd only spent a few hours with her but there was just something about Genevieve that made Walker calm. He wasn't anxious around her, and things he said just came out *right*. He felt like he hadn't just met a new girl tonight, he'd met a new *him*. He liked who he was when he was with her.

Walker pulled his shirt back on and turned to her with a big dumb smile on his face. "That was…"

Genevieve smiled. She was pretty content herself and didn't want Walker to ruin the moment. "Yeah, I know," she said. "Come on."

She took him by the hand to head back down to the party but he stopped her.

"Wait. Can't we just stay up here for a while?"

She looked at him gazing off into the distance. The city lights *were* pretty amazing.

She smiled again and wrapped her arms around him.

The Camaro slowly cruised down the nearly-abandoned John Street.

Suddenly, Sal saw something. "What's going on over there?"

It was some young people walking where only homeless people or serial killers dared to tread. The Camaro closely followed the trail of kids. They were all walking toward a small intersecting street.

"Hey, wait a second," Anthony said, trying to jog his memory. "The one kid said something about a party…"

Sal stopped the car. Anthony looked up and barely made out the sign on the unlit street.

"… on Front Street!"

The brothers looked at each other and broke out in big smiles.

Noah walked around, looking for Sarah. But there *were* over a thousand people in the crowd.

Noah was desperate. He called out, "Sarah! Sarah!" but his voice could barely be heard a few feet away, let alone by the other eleven hundred party-goers.

Noah looked around. It was hopeless.

In actuality, Sarah was only sixty or sixty-five feet away, dancing with Kim Striker, but a sea of people separated her from Noah. And from the way she was dancing, it looked like she was pretty into her date for the evening.

Pike wanted to check out the party and agreed to meet Dylan back at the bar in twenty minutes. He wandered around until he came to an area where people were covering themselves in paint and rubbing themselves on a huge canvas on the ground, like finger painting but with their whole bodies. After the party, the canvas was to be auctioned off for charity, but the goopy, sticky kids on the canvas couldn't have cared less. It was just incredibly fun. Pike was immediately in love with the idea, and even let out a spontaneous, "Wicked."

He grabbed a can of yellow paint and poured it over his head. One girl on the canvas saw this and laughed, but Pike didn't care. He plopped down onto a blank part of the canvas and started making "snow angels."

"I'm a bird! A pretty yellow bird!" Pike shouted out with glee.

Pike stood up to check out his work. Not bad. But it needed some red.

Pike went over, grabbed a can of red paint, and poured it on his crotch. He plopped down, facing the canvas this time, and started to hump the pretty yellow bird. A dude nearby saw this and cheered him on, "That's right, fuck the shit out of it, man!"

Pike laughed then stopped suddenly. Something was happening. He looked down.

His dick was getting hard. Realizing the irony, Pike screamed out, "Fuck!"

Depressed once again, he got up and went under the port-o-shower that was set up to wash off the paint (which thankfully was washable). He dried off his hair with a towel from a nearby stand and started back to find Dylan at the bar. But the party was much more crowded the closer he got to the bar and Pike soon found himself shoulder to shoulder with a ton of people. He bumped into one Asian dude on his cell phone.

"Sorry, man."

He looked up, making eye contact for a second.

It was the busboy.

"My cell phone!" Pike gasped.

The busboy ran.

Pike chased after him. They ran through the crowd, pushing people over, knocking others out of the way, and generally making a scene until the busboy broke free of the bottleneck and made a dash for the back loading dock. Pike booked after him, and after only a couple of seconds, he caught up to the busboy, grabbing the kid by his collar and throwing him up against the wall.

"Give it up," Pike demanded.

The busboy held out Pike's phone with his finger on a button.

"Stop or I'll hit send," he threatened.

Pike raised an eyebrow. "Wait, you speak English?"

"Of course I speak English, asshole."

Pike shook his head, annoyed. He repeated, "Give me my phone."

The busboy threatened once more, "I am sending a jpeg of a bag of weed to your mom as we speak."

Pike was confused. He'd deduced how the guy had found the picture of the pot on his phone, but asked, "How do you know my mom's number?!"

"Speed dial one, 'Mom,'" he explained, then added, "Aw, that's so nice you put your mom on speed dial one."

Pike loosened his grip on the kid's collar a bit. Amazingly, after all these years, Pike's parents still had no idea Pike was a stoner, and they were actually pretty strict. "Okay, okay, hold up. What do you want?"

"Give me the weed."

"Sorry, it already got stolen."

"Bullshit."

"It's true," Pike said with the utmost sincerity.

The busboy looked disappointed. "Fine, then I guess I'm keeping the phone."

Pike had had enough of all the bullshit and suddenly found himself without the will to keep arguing with this guy. "Fine. Keep it," he said as he let him go.

The busboy brushed himself off and pocketed the phone.

Pike turned to leave, then stopped. Something dawned on him. He turned back to the busboy.

"Wait a second. My phone doesn't have a *speed dial.*" It was a brand new BlackBerry, not a piece of shit Nokia from 2007.

Their eyes met. Busted.

The busboy ran and quickly disappeared in the crowd. He was gone.

Pike screamed out once again, "Fuck."

Tonight was not his night, he thought. It occurred to him in that moment that everything that had gone wrong had been a direct result of Pike being stoned. Maybe Dylan had a point about easing up on the pot.

Pike hung his head low and was just about to start back to the bar when he heard...

"Pike?"

He turned. It was Walker, with Genevieve.

"Hey, you made it!" Walker boomed excitedly. He looked around. "What happened to Haley?"

"I don't want to talk about it."

Pike noticed Walker was holding Genevieve's hand. Then he looked at Walker's face and stared into his eyes. Something was different. A disturbance in the Force.

Walker had gotten laid.

Pike knew, and without a word passing between them, Walker knew he knew. Walker blushed a little.

But there was nothing to be embarrassed about. Pike smiled and patted Walker on the back, genuinely happy for him.

A thought sprang up in Pike's addled brain. Even after all the shit he'd been through tonight, seeing Walker with that glow, that confidence and knowing maturity washed over his face... somehow that made it all worth it. He knew that one thing had nothing to do with the other. Or did it? Whatever the answer, in that moment Pike felt that all was right in the world.

"Come on," Pike said as all the negativity left his body. "Let's go find the guys."

———————————

Dylan stood at the bar alone, watching the talent walk by, but he wasn't in the mood for any more female companionship tonight. He ordered another beer from the bartender.

"Dylan?"

He turned and saw someone he knew. It was his friend Pete, the one who told him about the party, the guy from the ski trip. Dylan couldn't believe it.

"Pete! No way!"

They hugged, then Pete asked, "You didn't have any trouble finding the party, did you?"

Dylan laughed. "Yeah, no problem at all."

Just then, a girl returned with a drink for Pete and he kissed her. With tongue. Dylan recognized her. It was the hooker from Houston Street.

"This is my date—" Pete began but Dylan interrupted him, "Yeah, we've met. Hi, Coco, good to see you again."

She smiled knowingly.

Just then, Dylan's beer arrived and he grabbed it. "Well, you guys have a ball," he said as he bid them farewell. Then he added under his breath, "Or three."

Dylan walked back to the place near the bar where he had agreed to meet everyone. Just then, Noah returned, looking defeated. "I can't find her anywhere. There's too many people."

Dylan hated seeing his best friend looking so sad and hopeless. He had to do something. "I've got an idea. Follow me."

Noah followed Dylan to the DJ platform.

The DJ was a hot chick with a blonde Mohawk. She was busy doing her thing but Dylan gently touched her bare shoulder and she turned to him. She saw he wanted to say something, so she took off one side of her headphones so she could hear him.

"Hi. Listen. My friend here needs to borrow your P.A. system for a sec."

And then he smiled.

The three brothers searched the party, looking for the dead men that had dared fuck with them. "They're here somewhere," Anthony told his brothers.

Sarah and Kim Striker were having a great time, dancing along to the music. By now Sarah knew that Kim was into her, and by the way she let him grab her ass and grind her on the dance floor she made it clear that she was into him as well. She wondered what it would be like to kiss him.

All of a sudden, the music stopped.

There was some confusion, some murmurs from the crowd, then...

"Excuse me," Noah announced over the P.A. system. "Sorry to interrupt the party, but I'm looking for my girlfriend Sarah Larson."

Sarah turned white. "Oh, my God."

Kim Striker looked at Sarah, a little ticked off, asking her, "Wait. You said you two broke up." But Sarah wasn't paying attention to him anymore.

Noah continued, for the whole crowd to hear, "Sarah? If you're out there somewhere, I just wanted to say I'm sorry."

He was talking into the microphone at the elevated DJ platform, trying to look out into the crowd, searching for Sarah as he spoke. "I'd really love to do this face to face. Are you out there?"

A hush fell over the crowd.

Suddenly, a spotlight appeared and started scanning the crowd.

"Sarah?"

The spotlight searched the crowd.

Sarah finally raised her hand timidly.

The spotlight zeroed in on her.

Noah's eyes lit up on seeing her. She had never looked more beautiful.

She called out, "What do you want, Noah?"

Another spotlight turned on Noah. And from somewhere else in the crowd, Anthony looked up at the DJ platform. "There! That's the guy!" Anthony shouted triumphantly. They lumbered toward him.

Noah continued, "Everything is changing so fast, I feel like it's all slipping away. But I don't want to lose you."

The crowd let out a collective "aw" and Sarah's heart was starting to melt as well.

"Who knows what'll happen when we go off to school, but why not spend the summer together? Maybe the odds are against us, but who cares? Why waste the time that we do have?"

Noah suddenly realized he didn't have to keep talking into the microphone. He handed it back to the DJ and headed through the crowd to her. "Excuse me, let me through, excuse me." The spotlight followed him.

Noah made his way through the rapt crowd and finally reached

Sarah as the two spotlights merged into one.

She was a little teary-eyed. "I thought you said we had to be realistic."

"But isn't that what high school is all about? Being unrealistic?" He took her hand in his. "Look, Sarah, I love you, and that's all that matters."

Sarah wasn't one to drag things out when her mind was made up. She kissed him! And the crowd went wild with cheers and applause.

The music started up again and amid the deafening noise, Sarah whispered, "I'm scared, too."

"I know."

They kissed again. Sarah suddenly realized that Kim Striker was still standing there and she came up for air. "Oh, so this is my friend Kim."

Noah shook his hand. "Hey. Sorry to ruin your date."

Kim Striker threw up his hands. "She's all yours, dude. No way I'm getting in the middle of this."

Suddenly, there was a scream. Noah looked back at the DJ platform and saw the three brothers dragging Dylan to the floor. Noah's heart sank. "Dylan!" He raced through the crowd with Sarah close behind.

The crowd of people had formed a circle around the fight and no one dared to interfere. Anthony and Sal held Dylan by the arms as Vinnie delivered a powerful roundhouse punch to the face. Blood splattered from Dylan's mouth.

In a fair fight, Dylan might have been able to take any one of them. But three against one was different, and even an experienced Army Ranger would have had a hard time fending off three hardened street fighters. Still, Dylan eked out a bloody smile, not willing to give them the satisfaction of seeing him suffer.

This further enraged Vinnie. "No one steals from us!" he shouted. Then he punched Dylan in the gut, doubling him over in pain and wiping the smile off his face.

But Dylan was treating this as a matter of pride. Or endurance. He recovered, looked up at Vinnie with a glimmer in his eye, and said, "Fuck you."

Just then, Noah pushed through the crowd and *tackled Vinnie*, slamming him into the ground. Sarah screamed!

The other two brothers dropped Dylan and rushed over to Noah who put up his hands defensively. "Stop! Stop!" he pleaded, and the guys stopped to hear him out.

"Look, we'll pay you the money. But you did steal our marijuana." Noah looked over and saw Pike and Walker rushing toward him with Genevieve.

Pike whispered to Walker, "*These* are the guys who stole my weed?"

Pike and Walker glued themselves to Noah's side and squared off against the three brothers. Noah helped Dylan up. Now at least it was a fair fight.

Each of the four friends had had an occasional fist fight in his day. What normal American boy hadn't? But this was different. Judging by Dylan's injuries, they were probably going to wind up in the hospital shortly. But in that moment, none of them was thinking about the consequences. They weren't scared, even a little. They were acting on instinct, an instinct that was telling them to protect their friend. It was a moment of pure camaraderie. They glanced at each other for a split second and smiled. There was no place in the world they'd rather be.

"You wanna do this?" Sal asked rhetorically, "Let's do this." He raised his fist, but before he could throw the next punch, someone grabbed his arm from behind.

He turned to see *Chuck* towering over him. And behind Chuck was the rest of the Hall High football team, ready to fight. Dylan and the guys broke into big smiles, elated that Chuck Zambrelli was going to save the day.

"No, *now* let's do this," Chuck said dramatically.

Fists started flying with the four friends in the center of the melee. It was chaotic, with punches and kicks flying from every direction.

Dylan took another shot to the stomach and fell to the floor.

Walker stepped in front of Genevieve to protect her.

Sarah and Noah helped Dylan up off the floor.

Then...

Blam!

A gunshot rang out.

It was Anthony with a gun.

CHAPTER TWENTY-THREE

THE REACTION WAS immediate.

Chaos.

A thousand party-goers began to flee the warehouse, screaming and shouting. The football team and the three brothers were swept up in the sea of people and Anthony was separated from the guys.

"You're dead, motherfucker!" he shouted after them.

"Run!" Noah yelled, succinct if a bit obvious. The guys ran along with the rest of the crowd toward the front exit.

Outside, kids were scrambling everywhere. The guys ran down the street to the Cube, Walker holding Genevieve's hand, and Pike, Noah, and Sarah helping Dylan. Even Chuck took cover with the guys, for lack of anywhere else to run to.

They reached the Cube and Dylan pulled out the keys. "I don't think I can drive," he moaned, still holding his stomach.

"Don't worry," Noah reassured him. "I got this." Noah helped Dylan to the passenger seat, grabbed the keys, and jumped in the driver's seat.

"In! In! In!" Noah ordered. Pike, Walker, Genevieve, and Sarah crowded into the back seat, while Chuck dove into the luggage area behind the rear seats.

Meanwhile, the tow lot guys finally made their way through the crowd and burst outside. Anthony pointed the gun at the Cube but there were simply too many people in the way to take a shot.

Noah started the ignition.

"Hey, everybody," Walker beamed, trying to lighten the mood, "this is Genevieve."

Dylan looked back at her and squinted. "Don't you go to school with us?"

"Wow, it is such an honor that you all recognize me after only thirteen years of school together."

Noah peeled out.

The three brothers jumped into their Camaro and took off after them.

The Cube turned onto Beekman Street, then Noah made another quick turn onto Fulton Street. But the other car was right on their tail.

Dylan knew there was only one chance to get away. "High speed test! Hit it!" Noah looked at him for a second with a little smile of appreciation, then floored it.

But the Camaro kept up with them and actually bumped their bumper.

"Faster!" Walker yelled.

Dylan, assuming Noah's role, read off the speed. "Sixty... sixty-five... seventy..."

Noah swerved onto Park Row and the car literally went up on two tires. But the Camaro was still on them...

"Punch it!" Pike cheered.

"Seventy-five… eighty…"

Up ahead, the entrance to the Brooklyn Bridge was rapidly approaching.

Blam!

A gunshot rang out from the other car.

"They're fucking shooting at us!" Chuck reported, in case anyone missed it.

"Take the bridge!" Pike yelled.

"No, the F.D.R.!" Genevieve corrected.

Noah saw a line of cars stopped ahead, waiting to get onto the bridge.

"LOOK OUT!!!" Sarah screamed.

Noah swerved right at the last second and drove into the oncoming one-way street. The Camaro tried to follow, but hit the center divider instead, *smashing into it at full speed*. The hood flew up and over the car, which crumpled from the impact.

Meanwhile, Noah was driving into oncoming traffic. He overcorrected and slammed on the brakes. The Cube spun out of control.

Some of the occupants of the Cube screamed. Some of them closed their eyes and prayed. Some of them even laughed. But during those seemingly endless seconds that the Cube spun 360 degrees in the middle of Frankfort Street at 4:02 in the morning, Noah thought about Dylan. They really were sharing a moment they'd remember for the rest of their lives. Especially since there was a good chance those lives were about to end.

But God was smiling on them once again, and just like before, the Cube just stalled out and came to a complete stop in the middle of the street.

Everyone sat there for a moment not saying anything. Then Dylan broke the silence: "Entrance ramp to the Brooklyn Bridge, ninety-three."

Everyone burst out laughing.

Noah turned on the ignition again and they drove off. The Cube merged onto the F.D.R. north.

As everyone started calming down and panic turned to excitement, they began talking about what just happened. "I thought we were going to die." "Did you see the other car?" "That was insane." "Oh, my God, wait until people here about this."

Noah just smiled. A sign ahead read, "Henry Hudson Parkway, Yonkers, Albany, Connecticut." Noah signaled and merged onto the road out of town. He looked in the rear-view mirror and saw Sarah looking at him, relieved. But more than that, she was happy.

Noah winked at her and she smiled back.

CHAPTER TWENTY-FOUR

FORTY MINUTES LATER, Noah was cruising up I-95. In the back, everyone was asleep, Genevieve on Walker's shoulder, Pike on Walker's other shoulder, and Sarah against the door. Chuck snored from the luggage area.

Up ahead, Noah saw the sign that read, "Welcome to Connecticut." He turned to Dylan. "You want to take over?"

"Nah. You're fine."

Noah continued on into Connecticut.

Dylan was more or less recovered from the beating and was feeling philosophical again. "You know your life is going to keep getting better," he told Noah. "This is just the beginning for you."

Noah glanced at him for a second. Another rare moment of Dylan being contemplative.

"For all of us. We're not going to be those guys who look back on high school as the greatest time of their lives."

"I *am* one of those guys, Noah."

"No, you're not."

"Yeah, well, I would have been. I don't have your brains or lofty ambitions. That's what the Army is about. For the first time in my life I'm scared, and I like it. I didn't want to just go to UConn and take over my Dad's paving company. I wanted to do something that matters."

But for some reason, this explanation just sort of ticked Noah off. "You don't have to join the Army to get away from your Dad. Fuck that shit. You can do whatever you want with your life."

Dylan just laughed. "Oh, my God. I can't believe you just said that. You sounded exactly like Mr. Cardellini. You should totally write that in my yearbook." He mocked, "'You can do whatever you want with your life.' Maybe you can add, 'if you set your mind to it.'"

Noah just laughed. "I'm gonna miss you."

"Yeah. Me, too."

And with that, Dylan rested his head against the door and fell asleep.

Noah reached Westerly, Rhode Island in no time. Everyone was still asleep as Noah pulled off the highway. Noah took surface streets for a while until the Cube stopped at a railroad crossing. There wasn't a train coming. No lights were flashing. But for some reason the car was stopped anyway.

After a few minutes, the car pulled forward and crossed the tracks.

Noah pulled into a driveway leading to a large beach house at Misquamicut State Beach and turned off the ignition. "Guys. We're here."

Everyone slowly woke up. It was morning by now and the sun was just coming up. The gang made their way to the front door of Marco's beach house and Dylan rang the doorbell.

In a few moments, Marco opened the door, wearing a plush bath-robe. He took a quick survey of his liquor-less classmates. "Whoa, whoa, whoa. Back the fuck up. I need one, two, three, seven bottles minimum. *Times two.* Did you think I'd forget?" Then he turned to Pike, "And you owe me a shitload of pot."

But of course the guys had nothing to give. And they were too tired to argue.

Marco looked them over. "Jeez, you guys look like shit."

And they did. The guys were covered in cuts, scrapes, bruises, and other assorted injuries (not to mention the remnants of fire extinguish-er foam, foam-pit bubbles, and yellow paint).

"Just let us in, Marco," Dylan sighed. "We've had a long night."

But Marco just scoffed and replied, "You know the rules, compadre."

They all looked at each other, like, *Seriously?* After everything they'd been through tonight, Marco's little games seemed so juvenile. So in-consequential. So high school.

But they still needed to get in, so Chuck stepped up to Marco and pulled something out of his back pocket. It was a little notepad, like the kind a detective might use.

"What's this supposed to be?" Marco asked dismissively.

"A list of every bottle that's come into your house since Freshman year," Chuck explained. Sure enough, the notepad had Chuck's hand-written inventory going back four years.

"Wow, that must have been a lot of work for you, Chuck. Good for you!" Marco mocked.

"Look, dickhead. If you don't let us in right now, this little note-book might just wind up in the wrong hands," Chuck threatened.

"What are you gonna do? Tell my dad?" From the tone of his voice, it was obvious that wasn't much of a threat.

Chuck looked defeated. He'd tried his best.

But then, Genevieve stepped forward. "Actually, we're going to tell the ATF."

"What the fuck are you talking about?"

"The Bureau of *Alcohol*, Tobacco, and Firearms," she explained. "Chuck's records are more than enough to get a federal indictment on illegal trafficking and distribution."

"Yeah, right," Marco replied, not so sure.

Dylan continued the pressure. "This is serious, douche-bag. You don't think they would care about your little operation? Let's find out."

Walker smiled and joined in. "You don't have a liquor license, do you, Marco?"

Noah was game, too. "You know the ATF will seize your dad's house. Both of them."

Sarah delivered the coup de grâce, "You think your dad might care then?"

Chuck smiled. He liked having everyone on his side for a change.

Marco looked them over. They looked like they just might do it.

"In honor of Beach Weekend," Marco croaked, "I think we can let it slide."

He opened the door and everyone came in.

"Oh, and I'm not paying you for your piece of shit couch either," Pike announced. He gave Marco the finger as he passed him.

Inside, the house looked semi-trashed, like there was a big party last night. No comparison to the party in the city, but still, it looked like they all had fun. Most of the seniors were still sleeping and they had made do without beds, sleeping on couches, in chairs, and on the floor in sleeping bags.

Dylan looked at Noah and the rest of the guys and smiled. They had gone off to New York as boys and returned as men. Or something like that. And maybe that was the whole point Dylan was trying to get across. One last hurrah before the unrelenting march of time changed everything. For the first time they were facing their futures alone. No friends or family to hold their hands on the next big step. And if that's what growing up means—going out into the world alone—then maybe it wasn't all it was cracked up to be. But somehow, after tonight, they were kind of okay with it.

The gang broke up and Pike pulled Dylan aside. "Hey, can I ask you something?"

"Sure."

"About what you wrote. In my yearbook. About 'reinventing my-self.'"

Dylan was listening. He was glad Pike had read it.

Pike continued, "I don't want to be 'that guy' in college. I'm going to try to quit smoking pot."

Dylan tried to contain a smile and just said nonchalantly, "That's cool."

"Or at least cut back."

Dylan patted Pike on the back. "There's hope for you yet."

And then something occurred to Pike. He said he didn't want to be the same old Pike in college, but that Pike was already gone. As much as there was no going back, there was no standing still either. In the course of one night Pike had *already* reinvented himself. Change was inevitable. And the thought of it—that Pike really could be whoever he wanted to be in the future—was actually pretty exciting.

Pike gave Dylan a big hug. Dylan smiled, and in that moment they knew what their friendship meant to each other. Dylan turned to head outside to the beach.

But Pike stopped him. "Oh, and one more thing. If a girl fucks you up the ass with a dildo, does that make you gay?"

Dylan raised an eyebrow. "No, of course not."

Pike cursed himself. "Shit. I knew it!"

Dylan just laughed and headed outside.

On the beach, Walker and Genevieve walked along the water holding hands. Walker was happy. The dawning sun lit up the Sound in orange and red. It was a beautiful moment. One, it suddenly occurred to Walker, that you usually only see in a herpes commercial. He tried not to let his mind wander and decided to stay in the moment.

That lasted another nine seconds before he blurted out, "You know, we should totally go back into the city some time together. Ooh, and I'm a really good cook. I could make you a lasagna some time—"

Genevieve covered his mouth with her hand once again. "You are the biggest dork in the world." She removed her hand and replaced it with her lips.

Back inside, Sarah and Noah were hand in hand. As they, too, headed out to the sand, they saw Dylan standing on the porch alone. "You know, you two make a really great couple," Dylan commented, truthfully.

"Thanks, Dylan," Sarah smiled.

"Here." Noah handed Dylan his yearbook back.

Dylan smiled. "I told you you wouldn't have time to sign it."

"I did sign it. We all did."

Dylan was surprised. "When?"

"Just read it." He headed out onto the beach with Sarah.

Dylan went over and sat down in a comfy lounge chair. He opened his yearbook to a page labeled "SAVED" on the top. He recognized Noah's handwriting.

I'll be honest, Dylan. I'm scared shitless. I'm scared about a new school, a new city. I'm scared about doing my own laundry.

Dylan quickly glanced at the page. It was filled out with all three of his friends' handwriting. He wondered when in the world they had time to sign it.

The answer, of course, was back at the railroad crossing. Noah had felt a surge of emotion and suddenly remembered Dylan's yearbook. So he stopped the car and woke up Pike and Walker. The three of them silently passed the yearbook back and forth, completing the message as one combined unit of friends.

Dylan continued reading, noticing that the handwriting had changed to Walker's.

But none of that compares to how scared I am for you. I was worried before about what we were going to do without you and now that takes on a whole new meaning.

Noah told them, he thought. *Good*. He didn't want to have to try to explain it again. Dylan continued reading as the message turned to Pike's scrawl.

I know you think you needed to protect us all these years and maybe you were right. But we'll be fine on our own. And so will you.

Dylan teared up.

———————————

The following weekend, Dylan went into basic training at Fort Benning, Georgia. They shaved his pretty emo hair but Dylan didn't mind. He strove to keep up with his platoon on a five-mile run, struggled to do another push-up in the mud, and strained as he repelled down a sheer cliff. And if that weren't tough enough, soon he found himself jumping out of airplanes in the middle of the night on air-assault exercises and surviving in the swamp for days on end with nothing to eat but what he could catch. He was pushed to his limit and he loved it. Welcome to Ranger School.

I guess it's time to grow up. We've known our whole lives that this day would be coming but now that it's here, it's just a little hard to believe. Not sure if we're ready, but it's happening whether we're ready or not.

In the Fall, Dylan's unit was shipped to Kandahar Province, Afghanistan. He'd seen some heavy action, but Army Rangers were pretty hard to kill.

On one mountain outpost, dressed in full combat gear, Dylan took a break, sitting reading his yearbook one more time as his unit ate lunch.

You were right about one thing. Life is for making memories. And we made some tonight. For that, I thank you.

Dylan smiled. Suddenly, a sergeant ran up and barked some orders. The men quickly stowed their gear. Dylan shoved his yearbook into his duffel bag.

Your friend, Walker

Dylan's unit moved quickly down a rocky terrain.

Your friend, Pike

The sergeant silently signaled a full stop and the men readied their weapons.

Your friend, Noah

For more information and exclusive content,

please Like us on Facebook at

www.Facebook.com/LastStopThisTown

or follow the author on Twitter

@DavidHSteinberg

Made in the USA
Lexington, KY
15 March 2012